Mrs. P. A. Hanaford

The Young Captain: A Memorial of Richard C. Derby

Mrs. P. A. Hanaford

The Young Captain: A Memorial of Richard C. Derby

ISBN/EAN: 9783337091897

Printed in Europe, USA, Canada, Australia, Japan

Cover: Foto ©Raphael Reischuk / pixelio.de

More available books at **www.hansebooks.com**

"I pulled off my boots, and laid my sword, pistol, and belt on a small board to push across."—P.—104.

THE

YOUNG CAPTAIN:

A MEMORIAL OF

CAPT. RICHARD C. DERBY,

FIFTEENTH REG. MASS. VOLUNTEERS, WHO FELL AT
ANTIETAM.

By MRS. P. A. HANAFORD.

"Sans Changer."

"Death is swallowed up in victory!"

BOSTON:
DEGEN, ESTES, & CO.
NEW YORK: O. S. FELT.
1865.

GEO. C. RAND & AVERY,
STEREOTYPERS AND PRINTERS.

TO THE MEMBERS

OF THE

Thirteenth and Fifteenth Regiments,

MASSACHUSETTS VOLUNTEERS,

AND

TO ALL WHO LOVE THE

STAR-SPANGLED BANNER,

THIS MEMORIAL

OF

One who Died in its Defence

IS HOPEFULLY INSCRIBED.

PREFACE.

—◦◦†︎⁂†◦◦—

THE biographer of the gallant Adjutant
Stearns gives, in his opening para-
graph, the very reason why the following pages should be presented to the
public. These are his words : —

"When a young man of promise has suddenly fallen in the presence of the nation and
in defence of its liberties, and all hope of
his future usefulness, in ordinary ways, has
been destroyed; if there was any thing in his
character and life, or in the circumstances of
his death, which, if known, might be of benefit to the world, that sensitiveness of friend-
ship could hardly be justified which should
withhold from his fellow-soldiers some fitting
memorial of him."

Justice and gratitude demand that I should
express here my obligation to the bereaved

v

mother of the young hero whose career of probity and honor I have attempted to sketch, for the efficient aid she has rendered by arranging materials, copying letters, and giving, in her own well-chosen and eloquent words, much information in regard to her son's life and character.

To the Library of the Essex Institute (in Plummer Hall, Salem, Mass.) I am also greatly indebted for much valuable material which is wrought into the following pages; and I take this opportunity to express my sense of the importance of that Association, and my best wishes for its continued prosperity; and also to thank all who in any way have aided me in presenting to the countrymen of Washington and Franklin this memorial of the stainless life and heroic death of a young Patriot.

P. A. H.

READING, MASS.

CONTENTS.

CONTENTS.

CHAPTER VII.

CHAPTER VIII.

THE YOUNG CAPTAIN.

CHAPTER I.

ANCESTRY.

"They that on glorious ancestry enlarge
Produce their debt, instead of their discharge."

YOUNG.

THE following pages are designed as a memorial of one who loved his country well enough to die for it. From the brevity of the life of its subject, and the scarcity of materials in the shape of journals, letters, etc., this little volume makes no pretension to anything beyond being a sketch of the life of a

11

noble young man, and a remembrancer
of a youthful patriot, who, *because* he has
died for his country, should live in the
hearts of his countrymen.

Believing with the biographer of the
lamented Chaplain Fuller that " to a reasonable extent, family history forms a
legitimate introduction to a biography,"
this chapter is devoted to an account of
the ancestry of the subject of this memorial. Rev. Dr. Thompson in his Memoir
of the missionary Stoddard says, " The
biographer of the late Dr. Wardlaw has
these very sensible observations upon
the honor due to a worthy ancestry:
'There are some people who say they
attach no importance to a man's descent
or to family honors, and despise those
who do. Perhaps they may be sin-
cere; but I cannot help thinking their
judgment in this matter erroneous, and

their feeling unnatural. "The glory of children," says the wisest of men, "are their fathers;" and I do not see why an honorable descent should not be valued, as well as any other blessing of Providence.'"

The Derby ancestors of the subject of this sketch were among the noted men of their times. The first of the family in America was Roger Derby, who was born in England in 1643, and emigrated to this country in 1671, removing from Topsham, Devonshire County, near Exeter, in the south of England, and landing at Boston, July 18, 1671, according to the town records of Salem, Mass. He resided for a time in Ipswich, Mass., but as he and his wife were non-conformists to the church of England, and of the Society called Friends, or Quakers, they were subject to various petty persecutions for trifling offences, till at last those fines, etc., were too grievous to be endured, and after ten years spent in Ipswich, they removed to Salem. He was, like the father of Dr. Franklin, a tallow chandler. The maiden name of his wife was Kilham. She died in 1689, but her husband lived nine years longer. "Their gravestones are yet standing, and bear the most ancient inscriptions now to be seen in the old burial-ground at South Danvers." * Roger Derby had twelve children, of whom the next ancestor of our subject was the sixth, Richard Derby, born in Ipswich, Oct. 8, 1679. He was a son of the ocean; but little is now known of his personal history, except that he was one of a number of pilots sent from Salem in an expedition against Port Royal in 1710. He mar-

* "Historical Collections of the Essex Institute," vol. 3.

ried Maria, daughter of Col. Elias Hasket, who had been governor of New
Providence, one of the Bahama Islands.
Eight children were born to this couple,
of whom Richard, born in Salem, Sept.
16, 1712, was the ancestor of our subject.

" He was an eminent and enterprising
merchant, and accumulated a large
amount of wealth." In his earlier years
he was, like his father, a mariner, and
was an intrepid and daring navigator.
" At a period when the mother country
tried to repress the enterprise of the col-
onists, and confine their trade to British
possessions ; when the straits were in-
fested by corsairs, we find this young
man venturing to cross the ocean in a
craft which would be deemed now
scarcely safe to run from Salem to New
York."

" During the struggle for the independence of our country, he continued sound and loyal to the last; and he it was who bravely responded to the demands of Col. Leslie to deliver up the cannon in his possession, which Col. Leslie desired to seize. 'Find them if you can! take them if you can! they will never be surrendered!'" *

His first wife was Mary Hodges of Salem, by whom he had six children. "It is said that the race from which she sprung was distinguished for its size. An anecdote is told of one of them, a young man, six feet six inches in height, who was captured by a British frigate. When asked if he was not remarkable for his height at home, he is said to have replied, 'I am the shortest of six brothers.'" Mrs. Mary Derby's son, John, was the owner of the ship Columbia, which

* " Lives of American Merchants," p. 20.

was the first to enter the Columbia River. The second wife of Capt. Richard Derby was Sarah, daughter of Dr. Ezekiel Hersey, of Hingham. She survived her husband, and founded the Derby Academy in her native place.

The second son of Capt. Richard and Mrs. Mary Derby was the next ancestor of our subject. His name was Elias Hasket Derby, and is remembered as one of the most enterprising and successful merchants of Salem. His son, of the same name, prepared an extensive memoir of this pioneer in the East India trade, which is published in Hunt's "Lives of American Merchants." He caused to be erected in Salem one of the most elegant wooden mansions, at a cost of $80,000 at the desire of his wife, and a fine garden was attached to it, which covered a large area, ending in a terrace

overhanging the river. It was finished
in the very year of the owners' death,
Mrs. Derby dying in the Spring of 1799,
and her husband in the Fall. Thus " man
proposes and God disposes."

Mrs. Derby was Elizabeth Crownin-
shield, of Salem, and they had eight children, one of whom was the mother of the
brave General Lander, and of his sisters,
the sculptor and the author. John, the
fourth child, was the next ancestor of our
subject. He was born in 1767, and was
graduated at Harvard College in 1786.
He was a successful merchant, and a Di-
rector of the Salem Marine Insurance
Company and of the Salem Bank. He
died of apoplexy, at the Salem postoffice,
while holding up his lantern to see if
there were letters in his box. He was
twice married: first, to Sally Barton, of Salem; and second, to Eleanor, daughter of

Dr. Nathaniel and Eleanor (Foster) Coffin, of Portland. This John Derby was the grandfather of the subject of our sketch. His father was Elias Hasket Derby, third son of the above-mentioned John Derby, who was born Sept. 1, 1796; was a graduate of Exeter Academy; was married in November, 1829, to Miss Mary Ann Ailen, grand-daughter of Major General Crane, of Canton, Mass. (The family of Hon. Timothy Fuller, father of the Countess d'Ossoli and Chaplain Fuller, were thus connected, as Hon. Mr. Fuller married a daughter of Major Peter Crane, a nephew of Gen. Crane.) One of Mr. E. H. Derby's sisters married Hon. Robert C. Winthrop; and another, Rev. Dr. Ephraim Peabody. One of his brothers is a physician, and is now serving as surgeon of the 23d Mass. Regiment.

Mr. Derby was for many years town

2

clerk of Medfield, where he was univer-
sally respected, and where he died in
December, 1840, leaving three children,
of whom the second is the young patriot.

With this sketch of his ancestry, con-
nections, and family antecedents before
him, the reader should be prepared to
find the young patriot possessed of intrepid spirit, cultivated mind, pure principles, indomitable energy, and inflexible
purposes of loyalty to government, and
devotion to the right. Had his Quaker
ancestor, Roger, or his slave-holding ancestor, Richard (who bequeathed three
slaves to his children in 1783), looked
forward to the present day, they might
have been greatly shocked, as they
beheld their descendant, the young patriot, pursuing his manly and heroic
course ; the one because he bore arms at

all, and the other because he drew his sword for the overthrow of slavery, and the establishment of universal liberty in our land : but probably if the great problems of our day had been placed before them, in the light of the Nineteenth Century, they would have heartily approved of the course taken by their descendant, "the worthy son of noble sires."

The family crest of the Derbys is thus technically described : "Derby, Earl of, and Baron Stanley (Smith Stanley) on a chapeau gu. turned up erm., an eagle, wings endorsed, or feeding an infant in its nest, ppr., swaddled oz, banded of the third." The motto of the Derbys is the same as one on the title page of this volume : viz., "*Sans changer.*"

CHAPTER II.

BIRTH-PLACE AND CHILDHOOD.

"Look up, my young American!
 Stand firmly on the earth,
Where noble deeds and mental power
 Give titles over birth."

MRS. CAROLINE GILMAN.

BOUT seventeen miles southwest from the city of Boston, Mass., in a picturesque region of country, is the rural town of Medfield. It was formerly a part of Dedham, and was incorporated in 1650, being then the forty-third town which had secured the act of incorporation. The soil is fertile, and is watered by

Charles and Stop Rivers, the former of which is peculiarly a meandering stream. In this town, before slavery was abolished in Massachusetts, there were many victims of oppression, and when the delusion of witchcraft sent innocent men and women to the scaffold, Medfield had her Goody Lincoln, who was accused of evil influence. Here, too, were the inhabitants exposed to the assaults of the inhuman savages, who loved to tomahawk our forefathers. On a cold Monday morning, the 21st of February, 1676, the town was fired by hostile Indians. At the first dawn of day, they set about fifty buildings in a blaze. The inhabitants sought refuge in the garrisons, but some were shot down on the way thither, and one, nearly a century old, was consumed by the flames in his own dwelling. There were about

five hundred Indians in this engagement, led by King Philip, the chief of
the Narragansets, who rode an elegant
black horse, and directed the massacre.

Here, in this now quiet town, was
born the subject of this memorial, on
the third of October, eighteen hundred
and thirty-four. He was the second
child of his parents, and had one sister
four years older than himself, and one
brother three years younger. The lat-
ter died when but five years of age, so
that for the most of his life the subject
of this memorial was an only son.

He was named Richard, and because
he was named for an uncle who had the
letter "C" added to distinguish him
from a relative who was also named
Richard, the initial was also added to
his name, but unlike the late Dr. Luther
V Bell, Superintendent of the McLean

Asylum for the Insane, who adopted the V in his name from a boyish fancy, that he might show as many initials in his signature as other boys,* he pre-'erred, as he said, to be "plain Richard Derby," and after the death of the relatives mentioned usually dropped the " C."

From his earliest childhood he was remarkable for his obedience and docility, combined with great dignity and maturity of character. His mother states, " I do not remember that I ever had occasion to reprove him more than three or four times; chastisement it would have been very unreasonable to apply to one whose supreme concern it ever was *to know his duty and to do it.*" This is not merely the record of maternal partiality. Others who knew him in childhood tes-

* Memoir of Dr. Bell, by Rev. Dr Ellis. Page 7.

tify to his gentle manners and noble nature. He always spoke the truth, cost what it might, and having early learned how to keep a secret, no threats or coaxing could induce him to reveal what he was in honor bound to conceal. His earliest Sabbath-school teacher speaks of him as one in whom there seemed to be no guile, and confirms the impression of those who knew him only in after life, that he was "an Israelite indeed;" one in whom the religious element was largely developed, and who early learned to walk in wisdom's ways, and found them paths of pleasantness and peace. On one occasion he was at the residence of this teacher, — a large, old-fashioned mansion, built in 1690, and to him a favorite place of resort, — and so sweet was his voice, so charming his prattling intercourse, that his teacher

took up her pen, and wrote, almost re-
gretfully, a sentiment suggested by
them. " My childhood never· knew
those sweet tones of innocence, which
strike upon the ear with such thrilling
interest from that little guileless heart,"
the circumstance of her writing the sentiment fixing indelibly the hour and her
infantile companion's tones, so that, although more than a quarter of a century has elapsed, she still listens to their
Æolian music with the ear of memory.

At the time of his father's decease,
which occurred when Richard was but
six years of age, he spent three months
in the city of Salem with his father's
relatives, and every summer afterward,
during his childhood, he passed some
weeks in delightful intercourse with
those endeared friends; and they now
hold him, as a boy especially, in delight-

ful remembrance. Under their auspices,
he gambolled on the shore of old Ocean,
visited the wharves of that ancient sea-
port, and watched with ever-increasing
interest the in-coming bark freighted
with wealth from the Indies, or the out-
ward-bound ship loosing from her moor-
ings, in order to speed away in search
of that wealth.

Those with whom these early days
were spent still remember with pleasure his unfolding character, the bud
which had such beautiful promise of
beauty as a flower. One of them thus
wrote to his mother, after his earthly
career was ended: " It is true, our
knowledge of him had especial reference to the season of childhood, but he
then gave evidence of so much character and nobility of soul, that we *expected*
from him the brave, resolute, and worthy

manhood which his short span of life has so entirely realized."

In general society, during his early days, Richard was modest to a degree that bordered on bashfulness, and sometimes so silent that he might often be thought inattentive, yet nothing escaped his observation. Few possessed a more penetrating eye to discern the character of those around him, and his youthful associates were almost instinctively chosen from among the better portion of the boys and girls in his vicinity. There was a peculiar naturalness about him, and he abhorred affectation in others.

As we have seen, a portion of his childhood was passed in Medfield, several happy summers in Salem, and the later years of his boy-life in the rural village of West Newton; all of them

places of interest to the nascent spirit
which was endowed with a dear love
of Nature, and early perceived

" Tongues in the trees, books in the running brooks,
  Sermons in stones, and good in every thing."

CHAPTER III.

SCHOOL-DAYS.

"A mind rejoicing in the light
  Which melted through its graceful bower,
Leaf after leaf serenely bright,
And stainless in its holy white,
  Unfolding like a morning flower."

WHITTIER.

AS may be well sup-
posed, Richard was al-
ways tractable in school,
a pupil after his teacher's
own heart. His earliest
school-days were passed
in some of those com-
mon schools which are the pride and
glory of New England. At the age of
fourteen he entered the Lawrence Acade-

my in Groton, as a pupil, where he remained three and a half years.

That the influences around him may
be better understood, it may be well to
refer to the town in which he then resided. It dates from 1665, and was
probably named by the son of Gov.
Winthrop (to whom and others it was
set apart), from the town in England
whence the Winthrop family came. At
the time of its settlement, Groton had
its share of Indian depredations. In
1676, it was assaulted by the warlike
red men, about four hundred in number,
and the inhabitants were obliged to retreat into five garrisoned houses. The
others were set on fire by the savages.
A few months after, the leader, John
Monoco, was taken, and hanged in Boston. Groton, then, had its history, and
the imagination of the youthful student

was doubtless often kindled by the associations of the past, awakened by visiting spots where the Indians once displayed their savage ferocity.

"No place could be better calculated than Groton to have an effect on the mind of a youth predisposed to the influences of Nature. It is a town of much beauty, though that is generally of a quiet character, and more calculated to convey dreamy impressions than to rouse thought into a duty." *

Here Richard read and studied, both in school and out of school, for " the work of education is not confined to the school-house. It goes on at all times, from the day of one's birth to the day of one's death. It is most vigorous in childhood, because *care* does not habitually ride with us. But the school-mas-

* Life of Amos Lawrence.

ter is then literally abroad, and has as
many shapes as places ; the face of ex-
ternal nature, the great utterances of
the forest, the changing aspects of the
heavens, the babbling of brooks, the
opening of the pond-lilies on those
beautiful sheets of water to which they
are as pearls on the bosom of beauty,
the sighing of the night-winds,— these,
and a thousand other things that might
be named, have as much to do with the
formation of character as matters of
more scientific description." *

And all these did their work in ed-
ucating young Derby.   Besides these,
he had the efficient aid of competent
teachers in the Groton Academy.   This
flourishing institution " dates its origin
from a joint-stock organization formed
for the purpose on the 27th of April,

* Amos Lawrence's Memoirs.

1793. Five pounds constituted a share of this stock. Three hundred and twenty-five pounds were raised by subscriptions, or shares, taken by forty-four individuals, all of whom were inhabitants of Groton, except four, who were citizens of Pepperell." The academy was incorporated September 25th, 1793, and in November was opened for pupils. In 1797, the General Court gave it one-half a township of land in Maine,—about 11,520 acres,—which subsequently sold for fifty cents per acre.

The well-known merchant-princes of Boston by the name of Lawrence, were, some of them, educated here, and in after years liberally endowed the institution.

A son of the celebrated Rev. Dr. Lyman Beecher — Rev. Geo. Beecher — was once a teacher in this academy.

At the time when Richard was a pupil there, it was under the care of Rev. James Means, a graduate of Bowdoin College, and a man of much ability. (He afterward served as a Hospital Chaplain in New Berne, N. C.; and died, while in the service of his country, in 1863.)

Of this academy Mr. Means once said, at a public meeting in Groton, " Situated as this institution now is, with its large funds, extensive library, handsome philosophical and other apparatus for instruction, in a flourishing country village of more than a hundred fine dwelling-houses, surrounded with some of the richest and best cultivated lands in the Commonwealth, enjoying an unrivalled western prospect, bounded by the grand Monadnock, petit Monadnock, Watatuck, and Wachusett, and embracing the smaller hills of Mason,

Temple, New Ipswich, and Ashby, with the villages of Ashby, Lunenburg, and Shirley, in the view, it must necessarily, under the prudent and judicious management of an efficient board of trustees and learned and well-qualified instructors, take an elevated position among the seminaries of New England."

When Richard entered this academy, it was with the intention of fitting for college; but, when his course was nearly completed, his health failed, and for a time he was obliged to suspend all study; and finally his friends concluded he had better direct his attention to a mercantile career. He had not been idle, however; and was already far advanced in his studies. Latin and French he read easily; and his teacher was wont to say playfully to him, that he had more

Greek verbs in his head than any other pupil.

After a long vacation for rest and to recover health, he again sought his books, and in 1850 went to Northborough, where he became a pupil of Rev. Dr. Joseph Allen, a man of saint-like piety, and a Christian teacher in that town for more than forty-seven years. Here Richard's soul expanded, while his intellect was also fed. In the genial society of his teacher and that teacher's family,* his early religious instruction was more and more like seed springing up. Favoring breezes here more swiftly wafted his soul toward the Saviour; and so much of his Master's spirit did he imbibe, that he was pronounced the *loveliest* scholar ever in that family.

---

* Dr. Allen's wife is a sister of the excellent Mary L. Ware.

After his death, the daughter of Dr. Allen, who was Richard's teacher in French, thus wrote to his mourning mother: "Nothing but what is sweet and pleasant can ever remain associated in our minds with him; and to us, as well as to you, his memory will be one of the precious things this life has given us."

In early childhood he had been consecrated to God by the Rev. Dr. E Peabody, of King's Chapel, Boston, who was his uncle; and Richard seemed, while yet a youth, to have chosen the better part.

It is a matter of regret that no records in his own hand-writing remain to testify in regard to his school-days; but they were certainly very happy ones, and were well improved.

The town of Northborough, where he

was residing when a pupil with Dr. Allen, lies in a beautiful valley, between the highlands of Marlborough on the east, and those of Shrewsbury and Boylston on the west. This town, too, had its early colonial history; and the grave of an unfortunate young woman, who was scalped by the Indians while she was gathering herbs in a meadow near the garrison-house, is still to be seen. Here, no doubt, Richard stood, and pondered over the merciless cruelties of those copper-colored barbarians.

After leaving Northborough, Richard studied book-keeping at Comer's Commercial College; and soon after entered the wholesale store of Plympton, Stevenson, & Co., in Boston, where he remained nearly four years.

Before closing this chapter on the school-days of the young patriot, it may be well to state, that among his instructors he had, for a short time, the privilege of numbering that first "teacher of teachers" in America, Rev. Cyrus Pierce, — better known to his loving pupils everywhere as "Father Pierce." Here was a mind he could but respect, a heart he could but love; and, under his tuition, Richard not only grew in earthly wisdom, but in spiritual stature. Father Pierce's one rule — *par excellence* — was, "Live to the truth!" and never had he a pupil who was more willing to adopt it, and make it the purpose of his life.

Another teacher whom Richard greatly esteemed was Nathaniel T. Allen, still the able and successful teacher of youth in West Newton, Mass., Mr. Allen's labors for the advancement of young Derby were doubtless "*con amore;*" for he well remembered, and sometimes gratefully referred to, the time when he was himself a pupil in the Bible class of Richard's father, whom he still pronounces one of the best Sabbath School teachers he ever knew.

Thus much of Richard's schools and teachers. But above all was he taught of God; and his school-days were not only days of intellectual progress, but of moral and spiritual advancement. He drank deep at the Pierian spring, but he drank no less deeply at the fountain of living water; and thus his school-days were such as to promote his future usefulness and honor.

Mention should here be made of his skill as a taxidermist, and also in sketching and in the use of carpenters' tools. His knowledge was not book-knowledge alone. He early learned to sketch with crayons; and family tradition states, that at an early age he was often found stretched on the parlor floor, diligently sketching until he had produced a large and excellent picture of a fire engine, which is now framed, and adorns his mother's parlor, a proof of artistic abilities of no common order.

Specimens of his skill as a taxidermist are evident in the same parlor, where a blue jay and other small birds stuffed by him are seen; and a large loon, shot by him on Charles River in 1855, has a place there also, in a glassed box prepared by himself, the bird being placed in a natural position on a mirror surface, which gives the effect of water. He labelled it as the "Great Northern Diver" (Colymbus Glacialis).

He was so expert in using tools, that he made for himself a bookcase while

in Groton; and an inlaid checkerbcard
and other articles, especially a handsome
knife-tray, bear evidence to his unusual
dexterity.

He loved music, and was somewhat
skilled in playing the flute. Often at
night he would ask his niece to play on
the piano, and sing, "Do they miss me
at home?" and he would accompany her
with his silvery-toned flute; and, when
away from home, he often requested
that the same sweet song might be
sung in memory of the far-off, only son.

CHAPTER IV.

IN THE FAR WEST.

" I travel, like a bird of flight,
  Onward, and all alone."   MONTGOMERY.

" There is a pleasure in the pathless woods;
   There is a rapture on the lonely shore;
   There is society, where none intrudes,
   By the deep sea, and music in its roar.
 I love not man the less, but Nature more,
   From these our interviews, in which I steal
 From all I may be, or have been before,
   To mingle with the universe, and feel
 What I can ne'er express, yet cannot all conceal."
                        BYRON'S CHILDE HAROLD.

HAVING from early life cherished a desire to visit our Western country, young Derby readily accepted the offer of salesman in the store of Clinton, Babbitt, & Co., Beloit, Wisconsin. This was a retail establishment for the sale of dry-goods. 45

Wearying of this rather monotonous employment, and still eager to see more of the great and growing West, he determined to relinquish his situation, give up all indoor business, and seek in the wilds of Minnesota, amid the rough scenes and labors of border life, the health and strength which is so desirable. Exercise, he presumed, would strengthen his physical frame; and industry, he supposed, would supply ·his wants, and perhaps sooner fill his purse if exerted in that direction than in any other.

As to the only son of Mrs. Sigourney, "the broad, green West was to him the star of promise;" and as that "Faded Hope" exclaimed once, "Mother, if you will permit me to have my grandfather's lands in Indiana, I will make a fine living from them, and take care of you;" *

* "The Faded Hope," by Mrs. L. H. Sigourney, page 215.

so young Derby often spoke of winning wealth from the prairie lands, to lay at the feet of those he loved at home.

On those boundless prairies he experienced a sense of freedom which was delightful, and the pure, healthy atmosphere was inhaled with intense satisfaction. Always prompt to communicate with his friends at home, he wrote to them many glowing descriptions of the beautiful scenery of Minnesota. Sometimes he would vividly depict a prairie on fire, so that one could almost hear the crackling of the dried grass as it was rapidly mowed down by the devouring flames, and see the forked tongues of the enemy as he advanced; or by night behold a belt of fire all along the horizon, and see, above, the dark mass of clouds which overhung them as an immense pall by day, assuming a horrible, lurid glare.

Sometimes he would speak of sunsets gloriously beautiful. You could almost see, as you read his letters, the orb of day descending the western sky, till at last the fiery circle disappeared, leaving a golden and amber ocean where it had been, while the evening shadows would begin to creep over his forest home. The eminences around would retain the brightness of the sunset hour for a season, then blaze up like an altar flame; and then the glory would depart with the dying day, as the twilight hastened on, and the stars came out in the slowly darkening heavens.

Anon he would refer to terrific storms which swept around his Western home, when the lightnings would flash with unusual brightness, and the thunder roll in long, continuous peals, such as he seemed never to have heard before.

While in Minnesota, Richard built a log hut, with his own hands, upon government land which he had secured for himself. During a part of his sojourn in this hut, he was alone ; but he knew no fear, and was contented and happy. President Stearns says of his noble son, whose life, like Richard's, was given a sacrifice for his country, that while on a voyage taken for his health, " out in the solemn solitudes of the ocean, where he could often be alone with the great deep, and the clouds, and the blue expanse, and the starry night, and the storms, and the Maker of them all, he consecrated himself anew to Christ, and learned that ' believing was simply trusting.' " *

From Richard's letters to the home circle, and from verbal communications made after his return, there is reason to

* " Adjutant Stearns," page 39.

believe that a similar quickening of his spirit took place while out amid those Western solitudes. As Headley says, out there "a man cannot move or look without thinking of God; for all that meets his eye is just as it left his mighty hand. The old forest, as it nods to the passing wind, speaks of him; the still mountain points toward his dwelling-place; and the calm lake reflects his sky of stars and sunshine. The glorious sunset and the blushing dawn, the gorgeous midnight and the noon-day splendor, mean more in these solitudes than in the crowded city. Indeed, they look different: they are different." *

· Earnestly alive to Nature's sights and sounds, Richard could have echoed the same writer's words as he wrote, "I love Nature and all things as God made them.

* "The Adirondack," by Rev. J. T. Headley, page 193.

I love the freedom of the wilderness, and
the absence of conventional forms there.
I love the long stretch through the forest
on foot, and the thrilling, glorious prospect from some hoary mountain-top.   I
love it; and I know it is better for me
than the thronged city; ay, better for
soul and body both. . . . . I believe
that every man degenerates without fre-
quent communication with Nature. It is
one of the open books of God, and more
replete with instruction than anything
ever penned by man." *

As already stated, Richard loved the
sounds of the country, as well as its
sights of beauty and solemnity; and could
he have met with the following description of one thing which he enjoyed, he
would certainly have quoted it as a rec-

* Ibid., page 167.

ord of his own experience, and said, "But
there is one kind of forest music I love
best of all : it is the sound of wind amid
the trees.   I have lain here by the hour,
on some fresh afternoon, when the brisk
west wind swept by in gusts, and listened
to it.   All is comparatively still, when,
far away, you catch a faint murmur, like
the dying tone of an organ with its stops
closed, gradually swelling into clearer
distinctness and fuller volume, as if gathering strength for some fearful exhibi-
tion of its power; until, at length, it
rushes like a sudden sea overhead, and
everything sways and tosses about you.
For a moment, an invisible spirit seems
to be near; the fresh leaves rustle, and
talk to each other; the pines and the
cedar whisper ominous tidings; and the
silence again slowly settles on the forest.
A short interval only elapses when the

murmur, the swell, the rush, and the
retreat, are repeated. If you abandon
yourself entirely to the influence, you
soon are lost in strange illusions. I have
lain, and listened to the wind moving
thus among the branches, till I fancied
every gust a troop of spirits, whose tread
over the bending tops I caught afar, and
whose rapid approach I could distinctly
measure. My heart would throb, and
pulses bound, as the invisible squadrons
drew near, till, as their sounding chariots
of air swept swiftly overhead, I ceased
listening, and turned *to look*. Thus, troop
after troop, they came and went on their
mysterious mission, waking the solitude
into sudden life as they passed, and
filling it with glorious melody." *

A few years previous, the free West

* "The Adirondack, or Life in the Woods," by Rev. J. T. Headley, page 198.

was the home, for a season, of Rev.
Arthur B. Fuller, the dear friend of the
young patriot; and, since both have
become accepted sacrifices on the altar
of their country, this oneness of Western
experience, ere the exciting experiences
of camp life, has been noticed as an interesting coincidence. It is said of Chaplain Fuller, that, in the Far West, " his
delight in Nature could be amply gratified as he rode over the level or rolling
prairie, with its beautiful flowers nodding
among the verdure, its occasional park,
and its broad horizon, regaled by the
melodious songster, the long-drawn strain
of the turtle-dove, the clouds of pigeons,
like the arrows of Persia, darkening the
sun, and made romantic too, and even
dangerous, by the prowling packs of ra-
pacious wolves;" * and the same could

---

* Memoir of Chaplain Fuller, page 58.

be said in regard to the subject of this memorial.

His hut was no savage wigwam : but though he had to cut down the trees himself to clear a spot for it to stand upon, and then reared it himself, it was a comfortable, civilized-looking tenement; and he arranged his simple furniture in an orderly and even tasteful manner, having with him books, pictures, and other signs of a refinement not always to be found in the wilderness.

A beautiful lake was included in the region of which he was owner; and, as it stretched away from the land immediately in front of his cabin, he used to say it would be his door-yard forever. Not fancying its Indian name, he changed it for that of a favorite niece; and it is now known on the maps of that vicinity as Lake Manuela. Here, in his lowly home by the lake-side, he spent his time in a manner congenial to his rural tastes, daily studying and enjoying Nature in all its wildness, fishing in the clear waters of his own sylvan lake, or rousing the timid deer and dangerous bear in the pathless forests or along the water-courses. When wearied with the hunt, or exhausted with his efforts as an angler, he would return to his little cottage, and " under his own vine and fig-tree, with none to molest or make him afraid," he would study books as he had just before studied Nature, earnestly, attentively, and with a relish which betokened " a sound mind in a sound body."

Nor did he forget to *do* good as one of the ways in which he would *get* good. Many miles from civilization, with himself, he found a family of poor children with no means for education ; and a portion of each week he spent in instructing them in the rudiments of knowledge, while with each returning Sabbath he proved himself still faithful to his God and Savior by calling their attention to the high truths of the gospel, and earnestly sought to win them to holiness and heaven. Often during his brief life was he seen as a teacher in some flourishing New-England sabbath school; but never was he more truly engaged in his Master's service than when he threaded those secluded woodland paths in holy time, far from the "church-going bell," to meet those young immortals, and care for their spiritual good. Angels must have looked with serene satisfaction on such a self-imposed labor of love; and the dear Lord himself awaited his disciple with the words, "Inasmuch as ye did it unto one of the least of these, ye did it unto me."

This poor family were from " the father-land of thought," and with their German accent the little ones would call out joyfully, when they saw their benefactor approaching, — " Mr. *Tierby* is coming! Mr. *Tierby* is coming!"

They were in circumstances of great poverty, sharing none of the luxuries, and few of the comforts, of civilization. Knowing the German custom of celebrating Christmas, Mr. Derby thought he would surprise them one Christmas Eve. So he sent to his Eastern friends for a variety of small articles; prepared a tree, and hung it with the presents; enjoying greatly the intense satisfaction with which his efforts were received. He knew all his life long, by a joyful experience, the truth of those words of the Lord Jesus: "It is more blessed to give than to receive."

The visits of Indians to his lonely hut should not be unnoticed. His habitation was in Meeker County, and the Sioux and Chippewas were the Indians who most frequently visited him. The Chippewas are now few in number,— only five families in 1854. They held thirteen sections of land, and drew a perpetual annuity from our Government of three hundred dollars. The Sioux tribe is much larger, and embraces many others. These Indians whom Richard saw were peaceably disposed; but he could not look upon these red men of the forest, and remember that they were melting away before the white race, without some emotions of regret. They have, some of them, noble traits, and the rights of all should be respected; but they are destined to pass away before a higher

civilization, and soon the mountains and
forests which their wandering feet alone
have trodden will know them no more
forever. They will live only in the
memories of their successors, as the
euphonious names they have given to
lake and shore and highland shall be
uttered by the lips of a seemingly
higher type of humanity, and fall upon
ears that shall hear in those names the
faint and far-off echo of the past, — the
voice of the Great Spirit bidding them
remember his copper-colored children,
and be sure that they walk in the
light of the truth, or they also may
pass away.

Eighteen months did Richard linger
in the forest home he had chosen, and
then the attractions of his childhood's
home grew too strong to be resisted.
He returned to New England, met the

anticipated hearty welcome, and spent the winter amid the comforts and luxuries of his early days.

In the spring came an urgent call to the West again. One of the gentlemen by whom he was formerly employed wished his assistance in a dry-goods store in Wisconsin. He once more set his face toward the setting sun, to his mother's regret, but with her blessing. By an unexpected mercantile change, he was thrown out of employment, and induced to return again to his log-cabin, and to resort to hunting and trapping in Minnesota through the winter. At this time he was not alone, but had the pleasant company of two young men from New England, to whom he became warmly attached

He never forgot his home friends,

even when forest life was a novelty to
him; and during this winter he used to
walk ten miles every week to the nearest post-town, where he always deposited
a letter directed to friends at home, and
never failed to find one awaiting his arrival from the same source. The remembrance of the delightful correspondence
he always continued with his loved ones
at home now adds to the poignancy of
their grief at his loss.

While residing in Wisconsin with his
friend Mr. Babbitt, he was accustomed to
attend the Episcopal Church, and was
an interested member of a Bible class in
the Sabbath School.

'It is greatly to be regretted that his
letters from the West are not now to
be found. His friends used to tell him
they ought to be published; but he,
laughingly, advised that they should

be used to make lamplighters. His journals, sketches, etc., were all sealed up by himself, when he went out to battle for the Right, with the request, that, if he fell, they should be burned without opening; which was faithfully done.

Two letters, only, relating to his Western life are to be found. In one of these, with a characteristic desire to assure his friends that he was comfortable, he has sketched the ground plan of his log-cabin, and proved that he has things "well arranged;" and he humorously relates to his sister his adventures as a cook, thus: "I'm glad to hear that Mary holds out so well: she's a wonderful girl! I've thought of her a great deal the last twenty-four hours, for I've made a batch of Indian meal bread. I brought up a

package of yeast cakes, and last night
I thought I would try my hand at
some yeast bread. I left the receipt
at Mrs. Cooper's, but I remembered it
near enough. I had splendid luck. It
was as light as any of yours, and not
sour. But there's nothing like a *covered iron pot* to make a nice crust!"

The other letter — to his mother — is
less "matter-of-fact," and after speaking of a variety of family matters, he
says, "A Boston dry-goods *drummer* staid
here (in Beloit, Wis.) last Friday, and
I had a long talk with him about Minnesota. He had just been through the
Territory, and was very much pleased
with the country, the people, business,
and every thing. He said if he was
coming out West to settle, he should
go there without hesitation.

"If I should like, and succeed there,

perhaps you would come too. If I shouldn't, I might come back to Massachusetts.

"What is the use of talking about things six months ahead, and borrowing trouble, when things might happen in a week that would make a complete revolution in our hopes and fears, plans and prospects?

> ' One by one (bright gifts from Heaven),
> Joys are sent thee here below :
> Take them readily when given ;
> Ready, too, to let them go.
>
> One by one, thy griefs shall meet thee :
> Do not fear a thronging band ;
> One will fade as others greet thee,—
> Shadows passing through the land.
>
> Do not look at life's long sorrow ;
> See how small each moment's pain ;
> God will help thee for to-morrow ;
> Every day begin again.
>
> Every hour that floats so slowly
> Has its task to do or bear :
> Luminous the crown, and holy,
> If thou set each gem with care.'

"These lines are from 'Household Words.' With love to all, I remain your affectionate son, Richard."

The hopeful, trustful spirit evinced by the use of the above quotation was ever a characteristic of the young man, of whose life in the Far West no more need now be said.

He returned to New England in the spring of 1859. A few months following were spent in rest and recreation. Several weeks during that time, he boarded with some of his maternal relatives, on the green banks of the beautiful Connecticut River; and, while there, resumed his favorite pursuit of hunting and fishing; and also made a pedestrian excursion to the Housac Tunnel, fascinating, by his genial manners, all with whom he met, and causing one to write thus to his already doting mother: "It is not the lot of mortals to be perfect; but let those, who have seen any faults in Richard Derby, speak of them. *I* have seen *none*; he is the nearest perfection of any person I ever saw."

He improved, also, much of this leisure for reading. He was a diligent reader, and always read more for instruction than amusement.

On his return, finding his bodily frame invigorated, he entered the store of Frost, Brothers, & Co., in Boston, as a clerk; and there sought to perform faithfully his duties, with employers whom he respected, and companions that were congenial, and who did not forget him when he was far away, serving his country, but who still repeat his name with an affectionate pride, remembering that his youthful brow is now wreathed with the un-withering bays, and that his heroism, and that of his compatriots, whose life-blood crimsoned Gettysburg, Fredericks-burg, and many another field beside Antietam, deserve, and shall receive, a nation's gratitude.

CHAPTER V.

THE YOUNG VOLUNTEER.

"How shall I aid my country's cause?
How help avenge her trampled laws?"

Mrs. CAROLINE A. MASON.

IN 1861, the great American Rebellion reached the climax of war. The guns of the South were pointed at the "dear old flag" of our country, and the echo of their discharge at Sumter called the loyal men of the North to arms. Among the many youthful patriots who then answered the call of the President was the subject of this Memorial. He joined the 4th Battalion of Rifles in Boston, and was speedily stationed at Fort Independence.

This fort stands on Castle Island, in Boston harbor. The name is derived from the fact that after a rude fortification built of pine trees and earth had become useless, a small castle was built, with brick walls, and with three rooms: a dwelling-room below, a lodging-room next above, and a gun-room over all. There was also at one time on this island a strong building erected for the reception of convicts whose crimes deserved the gallows; but through governmental leniency they were permitted to be banished to this place. The island belongs to the United States, by which the fort was erected on the castle ruins.

While Private Derby was at this fort, on one bright and lovely Sabbath, he was permitted to attend divine services, at which his friend, Rev. Arthur B. Fuller, assisted by Rev. N. M. Gaylord, officiated. His beloved mother was also present. The Boston *Journal* reported the highly interesting services, and said : "After singing 'America,' in which the soldiers heartily joined, prayer was offered, and Mr. Fuller preached a discourse, selecting the words of his text from Luke iii. 14 : 'And the soldiers likewise demanded of him, saying, And what shall we do? And he said unto them, Do violence to no man, neither accuse any falsely ; and be content with your wages.' This, the preacher said, seemed to him proof that the Bible does not condemn a war that is waged in a good cause. The words of the text were intended to apply to illegal violence. He called especial attention to that portion of the text with reference to the soldier's recompense.

The reward is ample. There must be privations; and the man who answers his country's call does it with this upon his mind; but he has his recompense in history, and the realization that he has done his duty in a good cause, and if he falls his name will be remembered and cherished like that of the lamented Ellsworth. It was an honor to those soldiers who were the first to hurry forward and save our Washington; as it was also an honor to have been one of the gallant band who first went through Baltimore: and similar deeds, commanding the highest praise, were yet to be performed. The cause in which we are now engaged is, as sacred as that duty which we owe to our families at home. In conclusion, the speaker said the soldiers should bear in mind that America 'expects every man to do his duty.'

"The members of the Battalion had been drawn up in a square before the officers' quarters to listen to the discourse. The sun, which had been shining with uncomfortable heat, was overcast by passing clouds during the services, making it very pleasant and comfortable for the men. They were then dismissed for about an hour, during which a copious rain fell. At half past five o'clock a dress parade took place, and was witnessed by a large number of people. The appearance of the soldiers on parade was excellent, and elicited the highest praise."

At Fort Independence, with his comrades, Private Derby remained, from time to time receiving promotion as a non-commissioned officer, till in August, 1861, he was commissioned by Gov. Andrew as 2d Lieutenant in the Fifteenth

Regiment, then in camp near Worcester. Thither he went immediately, rejoicing in the prospect of more active service. The regiment was soon ordered to the South. The first letter from the young volunteer, after taking up the line of march, was as follows: —

"New York, Friday morning, Aug. 10, 1861.

" My dear Mother, — We struck camp yesterday afternoon, and marched to Worcester; and, after parading an hour there, we took the cars about 5 o'clock, and reached Norwich at 1 a. m. We went aboard the steamer Connecticut, and most of us had a good sleep. The officers had a good supper (by paying for it) and state-rooms, but some of the men neglected to put food in their haversacks, and had to go hungry, as the cooked rations were sent on in another train. We are waiting now on the wharf, and expect every moment to march up

to the Park, where we shall have breakfast. Lieut. Taft is ill this morning:
Capt. P. thinks he is threatened with a
fever. For myself, I never felt better."

"Aboard Steamer Transport, 6 o'clock, P. M.

"We did not go up town after all, but
waited on the wharf, and made a dinner
of ham and crackers. We are now on
our way to Amboy, to take the cars for
Philadelphia. Lieut. Taft has remained
behind in New York, with some friends,
on a furlough of three days, to rejoin us
afterwards, if far enough recovered. It
will be a night's ride to Philadelphia,
and nothing worth adding probably, so
I shall mail this at Amboy, if possible.
Love to all.

"From your affectionate son,

"Richard.

"I shall expect a letter at Harper's
Ferry."

This *first* letter from the young volunteer under marching orders, is, as may be seen, only the statement, of a dutiful son to an anxious mother, in regard to his locality and the means of comfort at hand. Most of the letters following are of a similar character, as might be supposed; for no expressions of patriotism were needed from one who had laid his life on the altar: and home friends are usually most desirous to know how the dear soldier far away is cared for while marching or in camp; and they know that their prayer need not be, " The Lord make thee strong and valiant," but only, " The Lord shield thee in the day of battle."

From our country's capital, to which city the 15th Regiment hastened, Lieut. Derby wrote again, dating at Camp Kalorama, Aug. 13th, 1861 : —

"My dear Mother and Sister, — We were to have marched from Washington City Sunday evening: but it rained in torrents for several hours; and we thought it best to remain in the halls, and sleep on the bare floor, as we had sent our overcoats out to camp by the wagons. I had a good night's sleep; and I guess most of the men had the same, they were so very tired. We marched at six o'clock, Monday morning, about two miles, out to Columbia-College grounds, and encamped on high land with the 14th Mass., two regiments from Wisconsin, and one from Indiana, and may be others. We are attached to Gen. King's brigade. We have made ourselves quite comfortable in spite of the rain. Our tent has a good board floor, and we have secured the services of a nice colored boy. He understands his business 'to the letter.' Fruit is abundant and cheap. Melons, tomatoes, peaches, and all kinds of berries, are brought fresh to camp every morning."

In the same letter occurs a sentence which shows his character as a good and obedient soldier. He says, "Some say we shall move to Harper's Ferry, which would suit me; but I don't worry in the least as to where we shall go, holding myself prepared for any move that is ordered."

Some of the romantic episodes of his Western life must have been brought to mind about this time; for he says, "I have been over to the Wisconsin regiment, and found several acquaintances from Beloit, and heard of a number who are in other regiments, most of whom are holding commissions."

We perceive how safe our soldiers often feel in camp by this sentence: "It doesn't seem at all as though we were

so near an enemy, so many of us together produces a sense of security;
but it is reported that the rebels are
encamped within eight miles of us.
We are still north of the Potomac."

Ten days after, he wrote to his
mother: "Every thing goes on smooth-
ly and prosperously. The 14th Mass. has
removed to Alexandria. We have pro-
cured boards, and built floors, kitchens,
sheds, etc.; but we may have to leave
them any time. The weather is very
rainy and cool, but clear this morning,
and almost like autumn.

"Cousin Haskett Derby has sent me a
letter of introduction to Gen. Lander;
but I have not presented it yet."

The reminiscences of his school-days
at Groton and Northborough were called
forth here; for he states, "I have discov-
ered one of my Groton school-mates in

Capt. Bowman, of Co. C. We had a great time talking over the Groton boys; and his clerk is Walter Gale of West Newton, or more properly of Northborough."

Only two days after, and they were called to leave their comfortable quarters; and on Sunday noon, Aug. 25, he writes: "We march this afternoon, at two o'clock, to join Gen. Stone's brigade, which, I believe, belongs to Gen. Banks's division: at any rate, it is in the direction of Harper's Ferry. The weather is favorable for us, — rather warm, but no dust."

There is a dash of quiet humor in the following, "My friends may stop that subscription for a silver-mounted pistol!!? as I have traded for one, and can shoot it with any of our officers."

On they marched, making thirty-one

miles in two days, and then encamped at Poolsville, Maryland. From thence, on the 27th, he wrote to his mother, "As near as I can learn, we are about three miles north of the Potomac, opposite the city of Leesburg, Va., and not far from 'Point of Rocks,' a name perhaps you may have seen in the papers. There are troops already encamped here from all parts of the free States. I suppose the object of collecting them here is to protect the passage of the Potomac at Edward's Ferry and thereabouts. We have seen or heard nothing of the rebels yet. We are up pretty well toward the mountains. I should think we could see thirty miles from some points. . . . . I am well, and not fatigued. I had a cold when I started, which I took sleeping in a *tent,* but was cured by sleeping in the *woods.*"

About a fortnight later he wrote, "Four companies of our regiment, including ours, are stationed on the banks of the Potomac as picket guards. We are living like Indians or gypsies in brush huts in the woods. We are watching the rebels on the opposite side of the river, who also have pickets thrown out in the same way. We see them every day; but there is a general agreement not to fire on one another, unless an advance is attempted, or reconnoitring parties sent out. The four companies are distributed along for three or four miles. Lieut. Taft is in Washington. I suppose he is permanently attached to the telegraphic corps. The captain has one platoon, and I the other, about a quarter of a mile apart; and, as he has charge of the whole department, in place of the major who is sick, most of the care of the company comes on me. The men like the duty very much. It is more novel, and they have but very little drilling to do, lounging around our bivouacs like Indians. Night before last it rained in torrents, and our shanties were no protection at all : it made some of the soldiers think of home. It reminded me of some rainy nights which I experienced in Minnesota. I slept soundly through it all, and did not take the least touch of a cold. We are not allowed tents, because it would disclose our position too plainly to the enemy ; and, for the same reason, we have no fire or lights after dark. . . . . My health is good, though I have had some trouble occasioned by the lime in the water, which is even worse than that in Wisconsin. I drink milk now altogether. . . . . What will Henry call his dog? Ask him if he would like to call him 'Hail Columbia!' I don't know of any thing that I really need that you could send me. It would be very pleasant, though, to open a little box of *knick-knacks* from home. . . . . I have written this in great haste, on my knee, just before dark, because I found it would be delayed four days if I waited till to-morrow."

On the 4th of Oct., they were suddenly ordered to pack their blankets and overcoats, and proceed to take possession of Harrison's Island. Lieut. Derby thus describes the change:—

"At half past four P. M. the order was received, and at five we were on the march. The island is about opposite where we were stationed before,—i. e., half way between Conrad's and Edward's Ferry; and between it and the

Maryland shore the stream is two hundred and fifty yards wide. The river has been high, and has just fallen, leaving a steep clay bank, softened to the consistency of butter, and overgrown with roots, vines, and weeds as thick as a hedge. We arrived after dark on the canal path, and found only one boat for us to cross in. It was a metallic life-boat, capable of carrying fifteen men, and was in the canal, from which we had to drag it to the river. The island had been reconnoitred during the day; but we were suspicious that it was occupied during the night by the rebels, and every thing had to be done with the greatest possible silence. The captain went in the first boat, and landed without resistance. I went in the second, and four more loads took us all. When we reached the top of the bank, a dirtier ninety men you never saw. Some of my men hoisted *me* bodily over the obstructions. On reconnoitring, all the human being we found was an old slave, who takes care of his master's plantation. He thought his time had come, and, falling on his knees, began praying fervently.

"Pickets were posted all along the Virginia side (two miles in length), and the rest of us went to sleep. In the morning we found that our quarters were very comfortable, as long as the Virginians would keep their cannon out of the way. The channel on their side is quite narrow, and in some places the bank is a bluff one hundred feet high, which gives them the advantage.

"We enjoyed ourselves all day looking round and eating fruits, vegetables, and chicken-stew. The colonel and major visited us during the day. After we had turned in for the night, the lieutenant-colonel arrived with a new order; viz., to withdraw all but thirty men (to be left as pickets) over the river to the canal.

That was executed in pretty much the same manner as last night. We all returned this morning; and now it is night again, and the same process to go through with."

Soon after, he again wrote from the island, as follows:—

" It is a rainy day, and we are making ourselves comfortable in the sheds of a ruined stable. We don't like to occupy the houses, because, if the rebels should see a number of men in them, they would shell them.

" Last night, at half past twelve, the report of a gun roused all hands. The captain and I started off to visit the pickets, and found them all right. The gun was fired on the other side, and was probably accidental. It was heard over on the canal, and the companies there turned out and were under arms in *three minutes.* The rebels seemed very

well satisfied to have us here. I think
they would like to have our troops cross,
and follow them into another Manassas
trap.

"I bought of 'Uncle Phil,' the old
slave here, the enclosed bill. That is
the flimsy foundation that the operations of the rebels rest on. The old
darky was very glad to get silver for
them. He had six or eight of them,
and sold them all. He said 'dat was
doing pooty well. I don't set no great
store by dat kind o' money; but it's all
dey's got in Leesburg, so I has to take
it.' He tells us a good deal about his
life, and it is as interesting as Uncle
Tom's. They all tell the same story of
the separation of families."

An opportunity for writing a few
pages for the press occurred while the
15th Regiment was at Poolesville, and
Lieut Derby improved it by writing to

the "Boston Journal." He did not write often, and finally ceased writing altogether, on account of the difficulty experienced in deciding what was and what was not "contraband" news.

The following letter is from the "Boston Journal," and is there dated Oct. 12, 1861 : —

"The first essential for pleasant camp life is an agreeable location; and ours is eminently so, being on a high and nearly level plain, where fresh air, sunlight, and beautiful views, are unlimited.

"Our regiment has had no experience in active warfare, nothing but marches, tiresome but not dull to the man who keeps his eyes open, the monotonous daily drills when not on the move, and tour of picket duty that had the spice of novelty to most of us. The Poto-

mac is guarded from Washington to
Harper's Ferry, and a part of that duty
falls to us. Four companies are de-
tailed at a time, to watch the section
between Conrad's and Edward's Ferries.
It is a six-mile march in the heat of
the day, but there is a prospect of fun;
and, for the first time, the men sling
knapsacks without grumbling.

"About a quarter of a mile from the
river, we come upon a battery of field-
pieces in a grove, crouching like a cat
for her prey. It is but one spring to
the ferry, if the rebels should show
themselves. One of our companies is
left here for its support. At the ferry
are two log houses, with curious-look-
ing holes in the walls; those in the side
next the river round and smooth, on
the other side irregular, and fringed
with splinters. The boys of the New-

York Tammany Regiment inform us
that they were made by cannon balls
that the rebels fired across the river.
One house was occupied at the time
by a family, which barely escaped with
their lives. Breastworks were immediately thrown up, and a few 'Tamma-
nies,' armed with Belgian rifles, keep
the savages at a respectful distance.

"The Chesapeake and Ohio Canal here
runs parallel with the river, from three
to six rods apart, but at a higher level,
leaving a wooded slope, on which we encamped, distributed in squads of thirty
or forty men for a distance of three
miles. No tents for us here; they would
be too inviting a mark for the bullets
of rebel pickets; but huts of poles and
brush, with an attempt at thatching
with weeds, serve for shelter from sun
and dew.

" The shooting of pickets is kept up.
There is a loose kind of agreement that
there shall be no firing except reconnoitring parties, and in case of advance;
but a picket sees a good shot, and can't
resist the temptation. Then half a doz-
en shots are returned to pay for it.
The distance across the river varies
from two hundred to three hundred
yards; but the marksmanship was so
poor, that only one man was struck.
Placing too much confidence in human
nature (if they are human on the other
side), he went down to the water to wash
dishes (men have to do housework here),
and got a bullet through his arm. Very
often, on a man's carelessly exposing
himself, he will be greeted by a sudden
whisk of a ball by his head. That was
amusing ; but the annoyance of our
lives was the army of bugs and spiders

that swarmed on our clothes and food; and now and then a four-foot snake would make us a call, generally crawling in over the pillows — no! — in the place where the pillows ought to be. A rich field for our naturalists!

"One enlivening incident was a night alarm. About midnight, the tramp of a horse on the tow-path arouses the sleepers. An orderly thrusts his head under the shelter: 'Captain, the countersign is changed,' and whispers a new one. 'What is going on?'

"'Nothing : only we are a little suspicious.' Hardly had we quieted down for another nap, when the same thing is repeated. This time it is, 'Captain, turn out your company under arms; the enemy are moving on Edward's Ferry.'

"So the men are roused, and told to

be ready for a brush. The pickets are warned to be particularly cautious, and the soldiers are permitted to lie down on their arms. The night passes without further disturbance, and all hands awake in the morning disappointed, and declaring that the 15th *never will* have a chance to fight. The next disappointment is the arrival of a relief, and an order to return to camp.

"One fact, to show the Rip Van Winkle class of people here. Our march was over the public highway from Poolesville to Conrad's Ferry; and when we went down, it was more like the bed of a mountain stream than a wagon road; but a fatigue party of fifty soldiers have been mending it, and it is much improved. It is the first work that has been done on it for twenty-five years.

"We are now impatiently waiting the progress of events opposite Washington, as our movements depend very much upon those of the grand army. The signs are very ominous; but silence, next to obedience, is the duty of soldiers, and I will remain silent till something turns up for me to write you.

"RICHARD."

To his mother, from Harrison's Island, he writes again, Oct. 17 : —

"I received the box of 'goodies' yesterday afternoon, with every thing in good order. . . The army songs I will give to the Chaplain when I see him. We are fortifying the island, and are to have reinforcements, and hold it in case of an attack. I was up till three o'clock this morning, overseeing the throwing up of entrenchments. The ruins of the old stone barn make a good fort."

Three days later began the disastrous

battle of Ball's Bluff, in which the gallant Col. Baker — a senator as well as soldier — and many other brave and noble sons of Liberty lost their lives. The Editor of the "American Annual Cyclopædia" thus describes the place from which the battle takes its name: "Ball's Bluff, or Leesburg Heights, is the name given to a part of the bank of the Potomac River on the Virginia side, east of Leesburg, and opposite Harrison's Island. The height of the bluff is variable, in some parts being one hundred and fifty feet. It is steep, with brush, logs, trees, and rocks on its front, and at the point of ascent was, on the day of the battle there, rendered soft and muddy by the passage of the troops. Opposite the bluff, and about one hundred yards distant, is Harrison's Island, a long, narrow tract of four hundred acres, between which and the Virginia shore the river runs with a rapid current. On the other side of the island, which is one hundred and fifty yards broad, the distance to the Maryland shore is two hundred yards, and the stream not quite so rapid."

General McClellan ordered a reconnoissance by General McCall towards Dranesville, and sent notice of the fact to General Stone, with directions to make a slight demonstration to start the rebels from Leesburg. General Stone immediately ordered four more companies of the 15th, under Colonel Devens, to proceed to Harrison's Island, to join the company which, with Lieutenant Derby, was already there. Troops were also ordered to Edward's and to Conrad's Ferries. The rebels perceived something of these movements, and a

regiment appeared from Leesburg, and
took shelter behind a hill, about a mile
and a half from Edward's Ferry.

"The day is Sunday, and at half past
four, P. M., Van Alen's battery of two
twelve-pound Parrott guns opens with
shell upon the Confederate force upon
the Virginia side. Their explosion can
be distinctly heard. Seven are thrown
within ten minutes, and no response
comes across the water. The direction
given to the shells is varied, so as to
find out the location of the force, which
is supposed to be concealed in a thick
wood to the southwest, on the hill. At
five o'clock, P. M., the battery in charge
of Lieutenant Frink, a quarter of a
mile from the ferry, also opens with
shell, and the two batteries keep up the
fire with rapidity. Just as the sun is
going down, the First Minnesota and

Second New York come down over the
hill, and take the road to the ferry.
The sun sets gloriously, his rays reflecting from the thousands of bayo-
nets which line the road.

"General Gorman is ordered to deploy
his forces in view of the enemy, making
a feint to cross the river, with a view of
trying what effect the movement may
have upon the enemy. The troops
evince by their cheering that they are
all ready, and determined to fight gallantly, when the opportunity is presented. Three flat-boats are ordered,
and at the same time shell and spheri-
cal-case shot are thrown into the place
of the enemy's concealment. Elsewhere,
all around, the air is perfectly still, and
the close of the pleasant Sabbath is im-
pressively beautiful; while the view of
the Virginia is almost enchanting. Soon

7

something resembling the sound of a drum-corps is distinctly heard, and the shelling and the launching of the boats induces the quick retirement of the Confederate force. Three boat-loads of thirty-five men each, from the First Minnesota, crossed and re-crossed the river, each trip occupying about six or seven minutes. At dusk, General Gorman's brigade and the Seventh Michigan returned to camp. The other forces at Harrison's Island and Conrad's Ferry remained in position. Here the movement should have stopped. The orders of General McClellan had been obeyed, and their object had been accomplished." *

The share which the brave and patriotic subject of this memorial had in this battle is thus mentioned by him in a

* The American Annual Cyclopædia, 1861.

letter to his mother, dated Poolesville, Md., Oct. 22, 1861 : —

"MY DEAR MOTHER, — I hasten to send you by the first mail a few lines, to relieve you from any anxiety about my fate. We have had a terrible fight; but I have come out of it safe and sound, except the effects of exhaustion and fatigue. We crossed into Virginia, and were driven back to the river, and had to swim it or be captured. Of course, I took to the water; but I had a hard time getting over. Captain Philbrick is safe also. He was struck by a spent ball, which only made a severe bruise. Co. H had a fight all by itself, before the rest of the regiments were engaged. Everybody acknowledged that we fought nobly; but, after fighting all day, we were repulsed, and I am afraid there is not half the regiment left. . . . Colonel Devens escaped unharmed, but the Lieutenant-Colonel lost his foot. They are burying the dead to-day, it being cold and rainy. I suppose the fight will go on to-morrow, but we shall not take part in it."

That Lieutenant Derby was brave and

faithful can be seen from the above extract, written with the unreserve of a loving son to an affectionate mother, whose sympathies he knew were for the Union and Freedom. In a letter to his former teacher, Rev. James Means, Lieutenant Derby gives more details of the Ball's Bluff engagement. He says, —

"The news of the fight created great excitement in Worcester County (Mass.), and many more people came on here than could be accommodated; but nobody blamed them for their anxiety, although they were really in the way. There happened to be unusual hospital accommodations, and all the wounded who were brought across the river received the best of care. Miss Dix has been up from Washington, and ordered a liberal supply of comforts. The wounds are all from gun-shots; and although dreadful to look at, only a small proportion are mortal. The weather is favorable for their healing. The fight was pronounced by all to have been a very severe one, and the ratio of loss was greater than at Bull Run. It is a mystery to me how *any man* escaped the shower of bullets that was poured in upon us for *two hours.* The pieces of artillery seemed to be the especial target of the sharp-shooters, and hardly a man was left standing by them after the second volley. I had always been afraid that the men would become unmanageable; but I was never more disappointed. Through the whole affair, from our embarkation in the miserable little skiffs to the retreat down the bluffs, they obeyed every order as promptly as though they were merely drilling, and fought as cooly as veterans. They showed the real English ' pluck,' and I think, if they had not seen that it was a hopeless and desperate fight, they would have added some of the French ' dash,' and carried everything before them. Early in the forenoon, Co. H had a skirmish on its own account with a company of Mississippi riflemen. We got the better of them, even with our old smooth-bore muskets, but had to fall back to the shelter of the woods on the approach of cavalry. Our loss was seventeen killed and wounded in that affair, and the same in the general battle. I went through the whole of it without a

scratch, not even a hole in my clothes. I
was very much disappointed, as some officers
had three or four bullets through their coats
and caps : so I made up for it by nearly drowning myself in the Potomac. I hadn't a suspi-
cion but what I could swim across with ease,
so I pulled off my boots, and laid my sword,
pistol, and belt on a small board to push
across. I was anxious to save my sword, as
it looked too much like surrendering to lose
that. I kept all my clothes on and my
pockets full. I pushed off quite deliberately,
although the water was full of drowning soldiers and bullets from the rebels on the top
of the bluff. I made slow progress with one
hand, and had to abandon my raft and cargo.
I got along very well a little more than half
way, when I found that every effort I made
only pushed my head under water, and it
suddenly flashed across me that I should
drown. I didn't feel any pain or exhaustion, — the sensation was exactly like being
overcome with drowsiness. I swallowed water
in spite of all I could do, till at last I sank
unconscious. There was a small island near
Harrison's, against which the current drifted
me, and aroused me enough to crawl a step

or two, but not enough to know what I was doing till I dropped just at the edge of the water with my head in the soft clay-mud. My good fortune still continued, and Colonel Devens, swimming across on a log, landed right where I laid. He had me taken up and carried over to Harrison's Island to a good fire, where I soon began to feel quite comfortable, but was afterwards taken sick, and have been till this time recovering. I should have returned to duty to-day, if the weather hadn't been so stormy. I feel as if it was in answer to the many prayers of my friends that I was saved at last through so many dangers."

To those who knew Lieutenant Derby, the closing sentence of this letter to his clerical friend is sufficiently indicative of religious trust and Christian faith.

To his anxious mother he wrote, Nov. 2 : —

" I am boarding in a private family in the village, but should have returned to duty to-day if it had not stormed so furiously. Capt.

P. drove me out of the tent, and said I must
go in doors to recruit, after my drenching in
the river. I felt quite ill for several days
after, but was not obliged to keep my bed.
I lost my sword, pistols, and belt, as did all
who swam the river. . . . I came out of it
better than some who threw away clothes,
money, and all. Captain Philbrick swam
across with his money in his mouth. Captain Bowman was a school-mate of mine in
Groton. We are now afraid he was drowned.
He could not swim, and made one attempt
to cross on a small raft, but returned. Some
time after, Captain Watson thought he heard
his voice out in the stream, and is afraid he
made another attempt and was drowned. . . .
General Lander was slightly wounded, and is
now in Washington. Those who are able to
travel are going home on short furloughs. . . .
Did I tell you that Lieutenant Taft is in the
naval expedition? We look to that for great
deeds. If that succeeds, it will lighten our
task on the Potomac. If it should fail, perhaps we shall have trouble with England and
France. I hope it is out of reach of this
tremendous storm. You must not look on
the dark side in regard to the war: affairs

are at this time looking better for us than ever before." ·

The naval expedition to which Lieutenant Derby referred was that of Commander Dupont, and consisted of eighteen men of war, and thirty-eight transports. They put to sea on the 29th of Oct., 1861, and, when three days out, encountered the terrific gale which Lieutenant Derby mentioned, and several vessels were lost; the crews, however, being saved by the heroic exertions of their companions on board of other vessels. The expedition was successful at last, capturing the forts at Hilton Head, and taking possession of Beaufort, Port Royal, and the adjacent country.

Lieutenant Derby thus continued his letter to his mother:—

"I cannot yet tell you wnere or what our winter quarters will be, but a few weeks will

decide. The state of the roads will soon put
a stop to active operations on both sides. We
have got a little stove in our tent, that makes
it as warm as we choose to have it. It is very
much like the one I had made to take to Minnesota. The thick boots and gloves will soon
be comfortable, and even necessary. . . . Our
Chaplain, Mr. Scandlin, is to have a furlough
in about a fortnight, and I wish you and Ellen
could see him. You would admire him, I
think. With love to all, I remain your ever
affectionate

" RICHARD."

Before leaving the subject of the
Ball's Bluff defeat, it may be well to
present from the " History of the Civil
War in America," by Rev. John S. C.
Abbott, a deserved tribute to the heroism and patriotism of the regiment to
which Lieutenant Derby belonged. It
is as follows : —

" On the 25th of October, the bereaved and
saddened remnant of the 15th Massachusetts

regiment, under Colonel Devins, held their
first parade after the battle of Ball's Bluff.
The heroism of this regiment, and of their
colonel, deserves especial notice. These Massachusetts men, deployed as skirmishers upon
the brow of the bluff, held the thronging
rebels in check for some time. Many of
them absolutely refused to go below the bluff,
but fought till they were shot down. It was
manifest that all further resistance was un-
availing, but these men would not consider
even the question of surrender. Colonel
Devins said, in his report, that under the
circumstances he would have surrendered to
a *foreign foe*, but that to traitors and rebels
surrender was impossible. The colonel himself swam the river by aid of three of his
soldiers. Upon the island he found thirty
of his men, and formed them in line of battle. Gradually, during the night, others
joined them, who had escaped. These were
the heroic men, but the shadow of the regiment which, but a few weeks before, left Massachusetts, who now were assembled for their
first parade after that disastrous day. Colonel Devins thus addressed them, in strains
which would have given a Roman immortality:

'Soldiers of Massachusetts, men of Worcester County, with these fearful gaps in your lines, with the recollection of the terrible struggle of Monday fresh upon your thoughts, with the knowledge of the bereaved and soul-stricken ones at home, weeping for those whom they will see no more upon earth, — with that hospital before your eyes, filled with wounded and maimed comrades, — I ask you now, whether you are again ready to meet the traitorous foes who are endeavoring to subvert our Government, and who are crushing under the iron heel of despotism the liberties of a part of our country. Would you go next week? Would you go to-morrow? Would you go this moment?' One hearty 'Yes' burst from every lip."

The battle of Ball's Bluff must be acknowledged as a Union defeat, but it was one in which those who were defeated displayed such heroism as to secure to themselves eternal honor. Rev. J. T. Headley thus refers to those battle scenes: —

"A rebel officer on a white horse galloped up to the Tammany regiment, and shouted '*Charge!*' pointing to the woods where the enemy was concealed. The regiment, supposing the order came from their own officer, gave a shout, and dashed forward, followed by the dauntless Massachusetts *fifteenth*, who supposed that the whole line was ordered to advance. A deadly volley received the brave fellows, and they fell back in confusion." *

Then came the retreat.

"The scene at this moment was fearful enough to appall the stoutest heart. Before the exhausted, bleeding band, rolled the rapid river; while, mingled with its sullen roar, there struggled up, from the deepening gloom, groans and cries and shrieks for help. Behind and above them, in the intervals of the demoniacal yells, came the plunging volleys, strewing the crimson shore with the slain. Still no voice called for quarter, — no white flag floated in the darkness. Overwhelmed, but not conquered, they disdained to surrender; and there on the banks

* Headley's "Great Rebellion," page 180.

of the Potomac, on that gloomy October night, were exhibited deeds of personal devotion and self-sacrifice, which have never been surpassed in the history of man. Men pleaded with their officers to escape; and officers used their right to command, to compel their troops to abandon them, and save themselves. . . . Opposite Harrison's Island, toward which the swimmers struck, the Potomac ran blood; for the bullets of the enemy pattered like hail-stones on the water darkened by the heads of the fugitives. Many a bold swimmer, struck by a bullet in his head, went down in mid-stream. Soldiers swam slowly by the side of their wounded officers, refusing, though repeatedly ordered to do so, to leave them. At last, the struggle, the flight, and the slaughter, was over; and silence fell on the Potomac, broken only by the roar of the torrent, and groans of wounded men that lined the shore and the bluff. Far down, over the rugged rocks, were rolling the lifeless bodies of the brave, whilst the living sat down in sullen rage, feeling that they had been led like sheep to the slaughter. . . . Not only was the fall of Baker, a gallant man, and senator of the United States, deeply lamented, but the destruction in the two Massachusetts regiments, composed as they were of some of the first young men of the State, was felt to be a national loss." *

Thus does this historian portray the thrilling events of an encounter which crowned more than one hero with immortal bays.

On returning to his duty, Lieutenant Derby again wrote to his friends; for, sick or well, he never forgot the fireside circle in his far-off New England home ; and, as his devoted mother stated, "always wrote in such a genial frame of mind, that his letters were like sunshine to the household now forever darkened by his absence."

Under date of Nov. 5th, from Poolesville, he writes : —

"MY DEAR MOTHER AND SISTER : — I am at home again, in camp with the remnant of Co.

* Headley's "Great Rebellion."

H, feeling as well, if not better than before
The weather has moderated considerably, and
made it more favorable for changing from indoor to tent life.   I escape guard duty for the
present (which is severe in cold and stormy
nights) by acting as adjutant till Colonel
Devens can send one on from Massachusetts,
where he has gone on a fortnight's leave of
absence to recruit the regiment.   Our adjutant has been promoted to be Assistant Adju-
tant-General of the 20th Regiment.   Colonel
Lee, Major Revere, Dr. Revere, and Adjutant
Pierson, are all prisoners in Richmond.   We
have not yet heard from *our* officers. . . .
Lieutenant-Colonel Ward intends to hold his
commission, and thinks he shall be *able-bodied*
with one *artificial leg*."

The many thoughtful and affectionate
mothers, sisters, and wives, who have sent
boxes laden with pleasant tokens of loving remembrance of the tastes and wants
of their far-off soldier friends, will appreciate the following extract from the same
letter : —

" The box arrived on Saturday night, in all the rain; but I did not know it till Monday. It was fortunate that you put so many papers at the bottom, as it stood in the water, and they protected the contents. The jelly leaked out a little, but did no damage: every thing was in nice order. The boots are just what I wanted, and the best fit I ever had: please tell my bootmaker so, if you see him. The loaf of bread was *very nice*, though not as good as if it was fresh. Several persons partook of it, and thought it very superior; and Wesley (our negro) wanted me to tell my sister that it was the ' *bess* bread he ever ate.' Thank your good Katy for her contribution: it forms a nice dessert. The stockings made Captain P. laugh, but they are just what I want for cold, windy weather. The cocoa is very acceptable, as I cannot buy any in Poolesville that is fresh and good: I had the paper of broma in my haversack, and I guess it is pretty well dissolved in the Potomac by this time. I see, by referring to one of your letters, that you want to know what I did for dry clothes when I got to the island. I sat by the fire till I got warm, and then I covered myself with overcoat and blankets, and kept

8

them on till I could change my clothes the next morning in camp by the hospital fire."

As a proof of the native modesty and good sense of the young volunteer, the following is given, from a letter to home friends : —

"Don't say any thing about my acting as adjutant, or I shall soon hear of my being promoted. It is only for convenience ; and the colonel expressly stated that it was merely temporary, so that there should be no misunderstanding. When Lieutenant Taft left us, one of my friends wrote me, that he was glad to hear that I was promoted to be 1st Lieutenant. Such things are very provoking."

Letters from old friends were always acceptable to him : so he adds, —

"If I don't hear from the store to-day, I shall wonder what has become of Burrill. When you are down that way, just drop in there, and remind them that I am not out of the reach of letters yet."

Our soldier-boys never forget Thanksgiving Day, though they may be far away from "the old homestead," and with no edibles suitable for its celebration according to time-honored custom. Thus Lieutenant Derby speaks of it:—

"MY DEAR MOTHER,—I have received both yours and Manuela's of the 17th. They served to finish off Thanksgiving day very pleasantly. We kept the day in New-England style. Captain Philbrick and I dined on roast turkey; and Mrs. White (the lady I boarded with in town) sent me a pudding as a present. We had a delightful day to celebrate in. Colonel Devens conducted the services in place of the chaplain, who has now gone East on a furlough."

That the young patriot kindly remembered all around him, when occasion offered, is seen in these sentences from the same letter:—

"I would like to have you get a silver lepine watch, to cost from six to eight dollars. It is for Wesley, our darky boy; and I want as good a one as you can send for that price. Have it put in good running order, and send two or three spare keys.* Also for myself two packages of brown stamped envelopes. If there should be a balance, buy some little thing for ' Katy ' and the children."

A letter written about this time by Lieutenant Derby, and published in the "Boston Journal," should not be omitted here. It is dated Nov. 23, 1861.

" TO THE EDITOR OF THE BOSTON JOURNAL, —

" The past week, although undisturbed by any warlike movement, has been one of considerable animation in ' Camp Foster.' On Monday evening, Colonel Devens returned from a fortnight's furlough spent in Washington and Massachusetts. The gratified eagerness with which the word was passed that

* Wesley's watch did not last long, for he carelessly dropped it; and then, as Lieutenant Derby wittily remarked, " It would not go, being afflicted with tic-douloureux and chronic rheumatism of the hands."

' the Colonel had got back,' even without his own confession, proves that this is in reality his *home*. One of the fruits of his labors while absent is before us already, — four hundred good rifles, to take the place of our miserable smooth-bores.

"Tuesday evening brought another welcome arrival, the paymaster, with brass-bound chests, little but weighty. A number of the wounded, who had been waiting for their two months' wages, were immediately paid off, and next morning set out, a happy party, for their homes in Massachusetts. Their furloughs range from two to six weeks; and as the four wagon loads rattled off toward Adamstown, many a man regretted that he too did not get a bullet, so that he could spend Thanksgiving at the homestead. But we couldn't get along without Thanksgiving in some shape; and considering our circumstances, the celebration came very nearly up to Puritanic standard. Colonel Devens manifested his fatherly interest in the happiness of his men by presenting them fifty dollars toward buying a good dinner, and the all-important roast turkey was not wanting.

"There was one feature of the day that I

take especial pride in mentioning, as indicating the *material* of which the regiment is composed. It is, that not a man was intoxicated during the whole day. What other regiment of eight hundred men, with pockets full of money, and plenty of whiskey within reach, can boast of so much self-respect and regard for their officers as not to yield in a single instance? You can depend on such men everywhere.

"Much anxiety has been relieved by the receipt of a full list of our prisoners at Richmond. We find in it several whom we supposed to be dead beyond a doubt. Our excellent Chaplain, Rev. Mr. Scandlin, is now in Massachusetts on a short furlough. Sergeant Jergensen of Co. A, who was wounded at Ball's Bluff, has received a lieutenant's commission, and is now in Worcester County raising recruits; and Sergeants Taft of Co. H, and Shumway of Co. E, are on their way there for the same purpose.

"The papers state that we have removed our camp one mile from Poolesville, and are settled for the winter in log huts. I hadn't heard of it before, and don't expect to, though the general impression seems to be that we shall remain here but a short time, but not go into winter quarters. We have enjoyed another week of Indian summer, which ended last night with heavy rain.

"Please ask the ladies to make the mittens with a forefinger, so that the soldiers can handle their muskets in them. How kind it is of them to attend to all our little wants with so much alacrity and earnestness! It makes another home-tie, whose influence counteracts the hardening effects of camp life. But I am getting toward *home*, and must subscribe myself, Yours, &c.,

"RICHARD."

Winter overtook the 15th Regiment in the same quarters. On the 2d of Dec., Lieutenant Derby wrote a letter to his youthful niece, which is transcribed to show his sprightly style of addressing his young correspondents. His winning, encouraging words and manner, in speaking or writing to the young, made his presence and letters always welcome.

"My dear Annie,—I received your note of Nov. 12th, and will answer it this evening, instead of writing to mother and Ellen. You get along very well at letter-writing. . . . Can you read my answers all by yourself? If not, I must try to write more plainly. I think it is a very good idea for you to keep a journal, if you try to improve in your handwriting, and in your mode of expressing yourself.

"Hoffman Collamore wrote me that you spent the afternoon at his mother's, and went to the Museum. Did you have a pleasant time? and what did you see at the Museum? . . . I shall be very much pleased to receive a pair of socks of your knitting. Mother says they are to be very nice ones. An old slave woman is footing a pair of legs; and, when I get them all together, I shall have a good winter's supply. We have not gone into winter quarters, as the papers stated, but I suppose we soon shall. General Banks is going to Fredericktown with his soldiers. See if you can find the place on your map of Maryland. We have built a log cabin for our guard to live in. It is very much like the one I had in Minnesota, but is roofed with straw instead of earth.

" Sunday morning, we could see the mountains to the north and west of us all white with snow; and the winds blew from them like winter. I hear that there has been sleighing already in Massachusetts. Have you had a sleigh-ride? Give my love to all, and believe me your affectionate uncle,

" RICHARD."

Thus simple and natural were his epistles to the children of his sister; for whom he ever felt a fatherly interest, and whom he sought, by example and precept, to train for usefulness. The letter to Annie was accompanied by a sketch of the guard-house.

On Dec. 15th, Lieutenant Derby writes from thence to his mother and only sister, —

" It is a leisure Sunday, and I may as well write home as do nothing but read. We have had a sudden change in weather from south wind to north; but still the weather is not severe. My friend Clark writes that there has been some skating near Boston, but there has been nothing like it here. We have a good board floor in both our tents, and a cast-iron stove in place of our sheet-iron one, for convenience in cooking. It is a cross between our ornamental parlor stove and a useful kitchen ditto. We had a joint of beef cooked in the oven to-day. The prunes which you sent were very nice. I told Wesley (our servant) we could have some of them stewed for supper; and he cooked them all at once, and served them up in our largest oval platter in the centre of the tea-table.

I will go up town some day, and see if the artist that keeps a 'daguerrotype shop on wheels' can take a miniature on mailable material. If he can, I will send you one. . . . Ellen is just a little too late for a lock of my hair. I had it cut only a few days ago, and that's why I'm going to have my picture taken now.

I still keep possession of my fork. It was in my haversack with my spoon and case-knife. I put them in my pocket before I took to the water. I will enumerate the articles I had about me while swimming, just for your entertainment; and you will wonder I floated as long as I did.

"The three items just named, my large jack-knife, horn pocket-comb, about a half-pound of gold and silver coin, a package of envelopes, a large memorandum book, a handful of bullets, a metallic box of caps, a flask of powder, watch, and all my clothes except my boots. I ought to have saved my canteen as a life-preserver; but I did not think of it, and threw it away.

"The report is that we are to have officers to fill the places of those who are prisoners. It will be a great relief, for we are very short for officers. The adjutant will take his place to-morrow, probably; but I shall not have to go on guard duty till I get through drilling the recruits.

"Prof. Lowe has been up here with his recon-noitring balloon, and made an ascension. I don't know that he made any important discoveries.

"I have consigned my *flying squirrels* to the company kitchen. They were unsociable animals, and troublesome to take care of. They very seldom made their appearance till after candle-light, and then scud to their nests the

moment any one attempted to make their acquaintance.   In company K, they have an *owl*
in a cage, and that is the *latest pet*.

"Our chaplain is still in Massachusetts.
He assists in recruiting, by delivering address-
es in the towns of Worcester County. . . .

"You musn't expect to see me home on a furlough this winter.   Officers are not allowed
leave of absence except on most urgent occa-
sions. I thought, from the tone of Ellen's letter,
she was hoping I should come home this winter.
Give my regards to friends; and with love to
all, I remain your affectionate son and brother,
                                   "RICHARD."

Three days after Christmas, we find
him again writing to a Boston paper.

"To THE EDITOR OF THE BOSTON JOURNAL, —

"We still linger at our summer residence,
with the prospect now of spending winter here.
But the past month has been so mild that I
could hardly realize it was December, till last
Monday, when the storm burst upon us with
boisterous fury. The sleet and wind battered
and rattled the canvas in a style any thing but
soothing to a nervous person. The frost came

in season to clinch the tent-pins, and save us from a general wreck.

"The surface of the camp streets and parade ground, that had become so smooth and neat, are covered with mud and hobbles; unluckily, too, just as the division inspector, Col. Dana, arrives, and we want to look our prettiest. Our new Sibley tents (conical) will do something to promote that desirable end. They are very neat in appearance, and make more comfortable quarters than any other pattern. Immediately after it became known that we were to winter here, the requisition was made, the tents drawn, issued to the companies, and pitched. Thanks to a live quartermaster!

" A bake-house has also been built; and the men now receive fresh bread, of excellent quality. Nothing is wanting to make them comfortable, yet they receive all these things as if they grew spontaneously. The quartermaster's is a thankless office: if he fails in the smallest particular in providing, everybody knows it, and pitches into him; and if he is always on the mark, nobody notices it.

" A gang of ' navvies ' are at work putting up a blockhouse in front of Harrison's Island, for

the accommodation of our pickets. It is built
of hewn oak timber, in the form of an equilat-
eral cross, sixteen feet on a side, and nine in
height, loopholed and roofed with earth to ren-
der it bomb-proof. It attracts a great deal of
attention from the other side, and they have
made themselves busy of late in erecting
counter-batteries. It must be a strong temptation to use their big guns, but nothing will
tempt them to fire a shot. Gen. Stone occasionally drives them out of their intrench-
ments, but gets no answer.

"Something has been done towards filling up
regiments. About one hundred recruits have
arrived, but we need many more. Pray don't
discourage volunteers before they get out of
Massachusetts. One of our non-commissioned
officers, who had occasion to visit Camp Came-
ron recently, reports that he fared worse, had
less comfortable quarters, and was treated
more roughly, than ever in the 15th. Many
are frightened out of enlisting under Gen.
Stone by the stories in circulation about him.
Half the lies that are told, if they were truths,
would have sunk him long ago ; and now they
have saddled the 'everlasting nigger' upon
him.

" I am well acquainted with the facts of the case, which gave rise to the report that he had returned contrabands to rebels ; and perhaps your readers may be interested in a brief statement of them.

" On the day of the battle of Ball's Bluff, the scouts of the Mass. 20th captured two unarmed negroes, and sent them to the Maryland side. They belonged to a Mr. Smart, who soon after wrote to Gen. Stone, saying he believed the negroes were carried away against their will, requesting him to give them permission to return. Just then it was not prudent to allow them to cross, but at a proper time Gen. Stone told them they were at liberty to go back to their master if they chose. Their answer was natural enough. ' Well, massa, you know a man likes to be where his wife and chillans is ; and Massa Smart allus been good to us, and I reckons we'll go back to him.'

" They went with the next flag of truce, but the rebels refused to allow them within their lines, and they were obliged to return to our side. Mr. Smart has the reputation of being a Union man, which probably accounts for the strange conduct of the rebel officers. Was there any thing in Gen. Stone's action in the

least degree illegal, injudicious, or inhuman?
While the *Home Guard* pick flaws in his management, he keeps about his business; and when
it comes to the fight, if officers will obey orders,
he will make a good commander.

"RICHARD."

Another letter to a young relative is
here inserted, as a specimen of his pleasant manner of imparting knowledge to
children.

"CAMP FOSTER, Jan. 19, 1862.

"MY DEAR NEPHEW,—I think you must be
looking for an answer to your letter of Dec.
28, and I will spend a few spare minutes before
it is dark in writing to you. If you were out
here, you would have a dull time of it. We
have a little snow, then plenty of rain, and
more than enough of mud, so you would have
to stay in the tent most all the time. I think
you would like the music that our band gives
us. They play three or four times every day,
and do it very finely.

"These little three-cornered letters that I
send you are orders that tell us what we have
got to do. I can tell you in letters a great

deal about military matters, so that you can learn something even if you do stay at home. What do you suppose the men have to eat?

"Every man has each day one and a quarter pounds fresh or salt beef, or three-fourths of a pound of pork; one pound of hard bread like crackers, or twenty-two ounces of baker's bread; beans or rice or hominy; sugar, coffee, or tea; candles, soap, salt, and vinegar, and sometimes molasses and potatoes. I don't mean that they eat soap or candles; but that is a part of what is called a ration. The quartermaster of the regiment gets all these things from the brigade quartermaster; and *he* gets them from Washington. Our quartermaster keeps the provisions in a large tent, like a great store; and officers of each company go there every morning, and draw what their company needs that day. The men's clothing is provided in the same way, and each man can have about forty dollars' worth a year; but if he needs more he will have to pay for it. The commissioned officers have to buy their own provisions and clothing. Do you remember that I wore, at Camp Scott, dark-blue pantaloons? Well, now we are ordered to wear *light*-blue, like the privates. A photographer

has come to Poolesville, and I think I shall
send you my likeness. You would hardly
know me in an army hat and overcoat, I'm
afraid.

"I hope you will keep on writing to me, and
write your letters *all yourself*, as you have
done. Give my love to your sisters, and both
mothers, and save some for yourself.

"Your affectionate uncle,

"RICHARD."

Nearly another month of winter had
now passed away; and still our young
volunteer is patient at his post. A letter
dated Jan. 24 gives an idea of his situation and feelings. He says, —

"I am keeping 'bachelor's hall' since Lieutenant J. left. . . . General Lander has gone up
somewhere in the vicinity of the 13th. The
victory at Somerset is a cause of great rejoicing. If *we* can't do any thing *here*, we are
glad to see somebody making progress.

"We are in daily expectation of marching
orders; but how it will be possible to move,
with the face of the country in its present con-

dition, I cannot imagine. But the 'natives' assure us there will be no improvement till late in the spring. We've had nothing but storm for nearly a week. To-night, for variety, we have sleet; and the wind drives it like pins and needles. The poor fellows on guard have a hard time of it; but that is a part of their duty as much as fighting is.

"I have bought a pair of rubber boots that reach above my knees, and large enough to admit of wearing two pair of socks; and now I can go through mud, and stand in the water with any of them. We have all donned the army hat, — an elaborate head-gear of lace and feathers, costing us ten dollars apiece. . . . . We had a funeral in camp this afternoon. A private of Co. G, who died of measles, which is getting quite prevalent in this regiment, was buried with military honors. It is a very imposing ceremony. The colonel, in the absence of the chaplain, reads the Episcopal service. The band and the muffled drums play a dirge as the procession moves to the grave, where three volleys are fired over the coffin by the escort, which varies in size according to the rank of the deceased. The inhabitants of Poolesville, who refuse to attend our dress parades and reviews, seem to take some interest in a funeral : perhaps because there is one more *Union man* dead and out of their way.

"I don't know how far Perrysville is from us ; but, if it were only *ten miles*, it is too far for me to visit Mrs. G. I am all alone now, and I don't like to leave my company for a day ; and leave of absence is no longer granted except in urgent cases.

"Ellen wouldn't like to have me try to grant the request she makes for a piece of wood from near the spot where I landed when I swam the Potomac! None of our soldiers go within at least half a mile of the place, and more than half the width of the Potomac to cross. No troops, either Union or rebel, have occupied Harrison's Island since the second day after the fight at Ball's Bluff; when Captain Philbrick, with a small party, tried to recover some tools left there, and the rebel cavalry forded the Virginia branch, and would have captured him if he hadn't retreated at 'double-quick.' I will try to find some little memento of the fight to send to Ellen.

"If you have not sent my box, please buy for me some kind of a simple game for two little boys, about seven and ten years old, children of a Mrs. White with whom I boarded in town. She has been very kind to me; and I would like to please her boys by a little present.

"I am writing, you will see, on very large paper, because it came handiest. My note-paper is running low, although I brought out a ream of it; but now Government furnishes more paper than we can use, and this is a sheet of it.

"I am very glad Manuela and Annie are skating this winter. It is an excellent exercise, if judiciously used. I haven't seen a pair of skates this winter, though they do have such things here occasionally."

With "stormy March" came orders to march again. The following extracts are from a letter penned at camp near Bolivar, Va., March 19, 1862 : —

"MY DEAR MOTHER, — I wrote you from Berryville, Va., and the next morning I received yours of March 7, which was the last; but we expect another mail soon. We marched the next day to within two miles of Winchester; and, before we had finished preparation for camping, were ordered back to Berryville, from which place we moved back to Bolivar, near the spot where we were stationed on the way up. We are entirely in the dark now as to our next move. All sorts of rumors are in circulation, sending us to all points, from Kentucky to Port Royal. They are taking away our teams, reducing transportation, and cutting down our baggage to almost nothing. . . I should not be surprised if we went down to Roanoke and joined Gen. Burnside. We have just heard of Burnside's victory at Newbern. We are getting so accustomed to good news that it fails to make as great sensation as at first ; but we are not the less pleased. . . . . I send a Confederate postage-stamp for the children's collection. It is a lithograph of Jeff. Davis."

In the above letter he says, " Captain Bowman is still absent ;" so that his former schoolmate was not drowned, as was feared.

The next letter in the possession of the writer of this sketch is dated at

Yorktown, Va., May 6, 1862, and, as usual, was addressed to his mother and sister. He says, —

"We have taken Yorktown without fighting. The papers, of course, give you the main features of the event. Sunday morning it was our turn to go on picket; but, before we got to our station, scouts came galloping in, announcing that not a rebel was in sight! We struck camp immediately, and marched over into the enemy's works, opposite our post, and camped again yesterday noon. At six o'clock last evening, we received marching orders; and after standing and paddling in the mud till three o'clock in the morning, advancing only about a mile, we were ordered to return to camp, and 'make ourselves comfortable till morning.'

"You can imagine what that would be after a steady rain of twenty-four hours, during which we had struck and marched and camped, and struck and marched and camped again. The army is in fine spirits. I never saw the men so enthusiastic. Every one seems to think now that we shall soon put an end to the war, and be sent home.

"The rebel earthworks are tremendous, — fort after fort of the strongest kind, and mounted with abundance of heavy artillery; but ours is so superior in range, that they could not withstand them. The guns which they make at Richmond are very poor affairs. Five of them lie here in fragments, burst by the overcharges in attempting to reach our batteries. The scoundrels buried bombshells and torpedoes in every road and all parts of the fortifications; so that, when we first entered, numbers were killed by their explosions. I had a very narrow escape from one. I went up to one of the guns that had burst, to examine it; and, a few minutes after, a soldier on the same errand trod on a torpedo, and the shell exploded, throwing him ten feet into the air, tearing off one leg, and burning him black as a negro! The papers report only *two* killed in that way, but there have been many of them.

"We are to embark on board transports for some unknown destination, probably West Point, and are now resting in line near the wharf. The army is in splendid condition. Everything is on the move. General McClellan is in high favor. It is 'Onward to Richmond' now.

" Save the enclosed circular. I found it in
the fort we have been besieging the past three
weeks. Enclosed I send sister Ellen a trifle,
which she can appropriate as she likes. Perhaps she has some pet object in view which it
will help her to accomplish."

In that last sentence spoke the thoughtful and generous brother; for whom his
only and beloved sister may well mourn.
Such rare spirits are always missed in
the home-circle, if not elsewhere.

Lieutenant Derby correctly stated the
enthusiasm of the army.

"Never did military expedition set out
under more favorable auspices than the Peninsula campaign in the spring of 1862. Victory
had perched upon the Union banner in a
series of momentous battles. Farragut's naval
achievements, transcending the rules of military science, as genius, and genius only, had
power to do, had sailed by the embattled forts,
and seized the Cresent City. This glorious
feat wrought up the zeal of the Union forces

to a high pitch of enthusiasm, while it dealt to
rebellion a stunning blow, and little was needed
to crush it forever.

"An immense army started to go up the
Peninsula, fired with martial ardor, and
flushed with hope. The enemy were in no
spirit nor force to resist its onward march.
But the great expedition paused before Yorktown, and, observing the most cautious rules
of military science, advanced upon the place
with the progressive parallels of a siege, as if
it had the strength of Sebastopol. But the
heart of the enemy failed them, and they evacuated. They were slowly and cautiously pur-
sued. They were vanquished in the battle of
Williamsburg; but advantage was not taken
of victory to strike an effectual blow. Slowly
feeling their way, the Union forces advanced.
The enemy meanwhile, by this dilatory progress, gained heart and time and re-enforcements. When Yorktown was evacuated,
Richmond had been almost destitute. But
time had been given to concentrate forces
there, and make fortifications. Within a few
miles of Richmond, the bloody field of Fair
Oaks was fought, and the discomfited foe fled
to the city. The rebels talked of evacuating

the capital, and all expected it to fall; but the Union army did not seize the occasion to attack it. Slowly approaching, the Federals came so near, that the clocks of the city could be heard in the Union camp as they struck the hours; and from a high tree, known as the 'signal-tree,' its buildings could be discerned.

"But the enemy had been re-enforced, not only by men, but by midsummer, which had been permitted to come upon the Union army, breeding pestilence in its marshy camp. This ally, in a heart-sickening, inglorious way, laid more brave Union soldiers under the sod than all the balls and bullets of the rebellion. The enemy soon made a concentrated attack, leaving Richmond feebly guarded. Now commenced a strategic movement, as it has been called; by which the Union army was withdrawn, badly shattered, to the protection of the gunboats. The right wing, as they retired, fully believed that the other wing was being hurled upon Richmond: but in this belief they were destined to cruel disappointment; and they arrived, weary and broken, at the riverbanks, to learn that the day was lost, the most reasonable anticipations of victory rendered vain, and one of the largest armies known to

history, composed of a rank and file of un-
equalled vigor and endurance, reduced to a
shadow." *

Chaplain Fuller, who was with the
16th Mass. Regiment in the Peninsula
campaign, was a friend of Lieutenant
Derby; and they were at Yorktown together, — the chaplain visiting Yorktown
after it was evacuated, while his regiment yet remained in the vicinity of
Norfolk. The chaplain thus wrote of
the encampment before Yorktown: —

"Three times have I visited McClellan's
grand and noble army. . . . The roads fearful beyond belief or expression; the uncouth
specimens of Southern 'chivalry,' and coarse,
vehement Secession women; the rich soil,
almost wholly untilled, and evidencing years
of agricultural neglect, — these have been too
often described by correspondents to require
any recital on my part. . . . I am stopping
at the far-famed Nelson House; which Lord

* R. F. Fuller, in his " Memoir of Chaplain Fuller."

Cornwallis occupied, while in Yorktown, in 1781. It is now occupied as a hospital; and in these rooms, which once were filled with British officers, and but a few days ago with Jefferson Davis, Magruder, and other rebel generals, now our sick officers and soldiers of the loyal army can be found."

But the chaplain and the lieutenant soon left Yorktown for the rebel capital. During the battle before Richmond, the 15th Regiment was under fire for three successive days. Previous to leaving Poolesville, Lieutenant Derby had been commissioned as 1st lieutenant. He was soon placed in command of Co. C; and early in August, 1862, a captain's commission was made out for him; but it did not arrive in camp till the word had gone forth, from higher than mortal source, —

"Soldier, go home: for thee the fight is won!"

His mother, whose anxiety during that

terrible Peninsula campaign may be imagined, but not described, received from him, at last, a letter dated "Harrison's Landing, James River, Va., July 4, 1862," in which he says, —

"I received your letter containing Annie's and the photograph last Friday, while out on picket; and since then I can assure you there has been little time for writing. We continued on active duty until Saturday night; when we deserted our camp, and commenced the retreat for James River. General Sumner's corps being the reserve, it became our duty to act as rear guard: at Savage's Station, we had something of an engagement, though I don't know what the loss amounted to. After dark, we continued our march; and, by Monday afternoon, nearly half our regiment had given out, exhausted by heat, fatigue, and want of sleep, — myself included among them. I was obliged to go to the baggage-train, and ride down here; and have not yet returned to duty."

To those who remember the slight

but agile frame of this young officer, it will seem surprising that he could endure so much as he did. His letter continues : —

" I am with Major Philbrick, two captains, and three other lieutenants ; all of us comfortable invalids. My stomach and liver seem to be out of order ; but now that we are out of the swamp, and have a chance to rest, I expect to return to the company very soon.

" The retreat was a tremendous undertaking, and cost us a large number of lives, and an immense amount of property. The fighting was continued for nearly a week. I was under fire for three days, — Friday, Saturday, and Sunday ; but the Lord sees fit to preserve me still ! The scenes along the line of the retreat exceed any thing that can be ima gined ! If the authorities would permit them to be described, no pen could give an adequate idea of them. When you see a ship-load of wounded landed at the Northern cities, you see comfort and perfect happiness compared with a field hospital, which must be deserted, and left in the hands of the enemy. The sick and wounded here are being cared for as fast as possible; but the rain of two days caused much additional suffering. I think the scurvy is prevalent, though not much is said about it here.

"There are plenty of gunboats lying here, which effectually prevents any attack on this point; and re-enforcements are arriving."

For a humorous conclusion of his letter, he appends the following postscript: —

"An old darky woman furnished us with an Independence dinner to-day. Bill of Fare: Stewed Hen, Hoe Cake, Farina Pudding, Strawberry Preserve; Drinks, — Muddy Water, Doubtful Tea, Whiskey Punch. Thanks to the Sanitary Commission for most of it, and a dollar to the old woman for the rest."

One more letter in a sprightly strain, and full of interrogations calculated to help the maidens in their reply, is here given: —

CAMP NEAR HARRISON'S LANDING, VA., July 19, 1862.

"MY DEAR NIECES, — I have three of your letters packed away in my box, which I think entitle you to at least one from me in answer.

" One of them (Annie's) I received quite lately, just before we left Fair Oaks. I was pleased to see the photograph of you and Manuela; but I don't think they were good likenesses: the attitudes were very stiff. I don't think it is a good plan to preserve such pictures, because somebody may see them, and think you really looked like that.

" Your Fourth-of-July celebration was a very successful one, I should think, judging from your programme and the account in the papers. I hope you enjoyed it as well as you expected to. I have often been in the grove where you had the picnic. When I lived in West Newton, I used to walk over there to bathe in Bullough's Pond; and that was where I learned to swim. Then there were no houses nor roads near; but now I believe there are quite a number of country seats on the hills overlooking the water. I would like to have you write me again, and tell me how you enjoyed the day.

" I suppose the summer term of your school

10

is ended, and that you are now having a long
vacation. What are you going to do to pass
off six weeks of dog-days? Do you go berry-
ing at all? Have you had any sails on the
river? What kind of a garden have you this
year? — both flowers and vegetables? Do the
fruit-trees bear well? Does Henry have a
piece of land of his own to cultivate? and
what does he raise? You may invite him to
answer that himself, and write as much more
as he chooses.

"What kind of stories are those you say
you write? I should like very much to read
one of them. You ought not to write any
that you know are poor: you should always
do your best. Do you keep up your interest
in postage-stamp collections? I send you two
of Jefferson Davis, and some of the larger
denomination of United States: I enclose
also a note of a South-Carolina bank. The
Jefferson Davis stamps and the note belonged
to a wounded Georgian whom we took care
of at Fair Oaks, but who died before he could
be carried to the hospital.

"There has been no fighting since we
camped here. The whole army is resting
and waiting for re-enforcements from the

North. Do you read the newspapers so as
to know what is going on in this country? or
do you think it isn't best to trouble your
brains about it? I should like to have you
trouble them enough, however, to write me
a nice, long letter as soon as you find time;
and with much love, I remain your affectionate uncle,

"RICHARD."

Harrison's Landing, the place where
Lieutenant Derby had now paused with
his compatriots in their retreat, was also
the temporary field of labor for his
friend Chaplain Fuller, who thus referred to the scenes there: —

"I have been at the hospital for most of
the past week, not as a patient, but caring,
to the best of my ability, for the wounded and
suffering sick of my own regiment, and the
countless number from the other various regiments of the loyal army, scarce one of which
fails to have more or less representatives here.

"The scenes one is called to witness here are
terrible. Ghastly wounds innumerable greet

the saddened vision; men sick unto death
with swamp pestilential fevers, make their
weak moans asking for pity and for succor;
exhausted soldiers, after four days' hard fighting, with scarce any food, plead for a piece of
bread, or they must perish with hunger; the
dying ask a word of counsel and of prayer,
and to transmit some message to wife, or
child, or mother, ere the last breath be drawn,
and the last sigh heave their panting bosoms.
The dead, too, lie on the earth, beneath the
sweet heavens; and their dumb, passionless
forms require, as their once spirit-tenants
have deserved, that those bodies, lately in-
stinct with vigorous life, should be decently
buried.

"Beautifully situated is this building where
we now are. The James River flows silently
by, its gleaming waters whitened with countless sails wafting supplies to the hungry army;
or else its placid face ruffled by the steamers
which come daily to the landing, bringing
hospital stores to the wounded and sick, and
returning down the stream laden with those
whose only hope of recovery or future usefulness lies in the revisiting of their homes, and
the solace of care and kindness there.   Lofty

elms line the avenue which leads to this dwelling; and the gigantic cottonwood interlaces its
branches with the lordly oak, though causing
its vigor to decay, and blighting by its contact. . . . Lovely as is this situation, it is
not more beautiful than the dwelling-house
which is in the centre of the town and its
skirting woods. The house is of ancient
birch, imported from England many years
since; whence also came the carved panel-
work and cornices in the rooms. President
Harrison is reported to have been born in this
house: so it has an historic interest already,
and will have more in the future. It is ele-
gantly furnished with rosewood and black-
walnut furniture. Fine pictures look down
upon you from the walls; and the library is
filled with costly volumes, many of them
books which have crossed the Atlantic ere
reaching here.

"Round the house cluster some twenty or
more whitewashed buildings, in which the one
hundred and twelve plantation slaves lived; if
theirs can be called life, and not existence
only. The owner of this house and all its
surroundings; the owner in man's sight, but
not God's, of all these human beings, — is Pow-

hatan B. Stark, M. D., now a surgeon in the
rebel army, and claiming to be a lineal descendant of Pocahontas. He fled precip-
itously when our transports lined the shores ;
carrying off to Petersburg all the household
jewels, and the most valuable slaves also, and
ordering the house to be burned by those re-
maining,—an order they did not see fit to obey.
He told such slaves as could not be hurried
away, that, if they were asked by the Yan-
kees whether they wished to be free, to state
that ' they are, and always have been, as free
as they wanted to be.' That order, too, they
have failed to obey ; but shout hallelujahs over
their deliverance from a bondage, which, though
not as heavy as usual, was nevertheless grievous, as slavery must ever be to the soul of a
man made in the image of God." *

On the 4th of August, Lieutenant
Derby wrote to a dear friend a letter in
which the following passages occur : —

"I have two double-letters of yours unan-
swered, which I had promised myself the

---

* Memoir, page 272.

whole undisturbed afternoon to answer, after
taking a long walk and a refreshing bath this
morning by way of preparation : but the adjutant comes down with the unwelcome announcement, ' that there will be a brigade drill
at 3 P. M. ;' which will probably upset both my
plan and my sanitary equilibrium. The rebels
say that this is the hottest part of Virginia,
and our drill-ground is the very focus of the
region round about. . . . We have had but
two events, of late, to remind us that we are
in the vicinity of an enemy. One night, about
a week ago, the sudden and rapid booming of
cannons and the whizzing of shells broke the
stillness of the night. The rebels had planted
a battery on the opposite side of the river, and
were blazing away at us with a vengeance. It
was some time before we got our big guns
to bear on them ; but we finally silenced them
without much damage. . . . Here is another
order : ' No brigade drill ! prepare to move,
—two days' rations in haversack, and sixty
rounds of ammunition :' so I must drop the
pen, and take up the sword.

" Thursday evening. — Here I am, seated
again quietly in our old quarters, after a
three-days' picnic. Our expedition was in-

tended to surprise the rebels at Malvern Hill,
— the scene of the great battle of July 1st.
Our division was to march round a cross
country, and fall upon their left flank, while
another moved directly upon their front. But
they were too wide-awake, and got wind of
the movement, so that they could withdraw
at pleasure. We marched most all Monday
night, taking a little nap just before morning,
and then advanced upon the enemy's pickets.
Firing began at daylight, and was kept up
pretty briskly for two hours. The 15th, with
its usual good luck, was in such a position as
not to be engaged, and did not lose a man.
Our post was an honorable one; and, if the
rebels had chosen to resist, it would have been
a bloody one. We bivouacked among the
graves of the killed of July 1st, — those of
the Confederates being single; while those of
the Federals were huge trenches, where all
were tumbled in promiscuously, and sometimes barely covered with loose earth. All
the buildings in the vicinity were *completely
riddled* with rifle and cannon balls. All the
inhabitants, black and white, had fled. One
rich old planter left so many proofs of disloy-
alty, that we burnt his dwelling and all his

out-buildings. Skirmishing was going on between our cavalry scouts and the enemy's
pickets, day and night. When it became evident that we had drawn down from Richmond
a pretty strong force preparing to attack us, we
had gained all we wanted; and, at 1.30 this
morning, we silently took our blankets on our
arms, and *left*, — arriving in camp early this
morning, tired, dusty, hungry, and sleepy.
After a bath, a meal, and a nap, 'Richard is
himself again,' and proceeds to refresh his
famished social nature with an epistolary chat
with the one whom he always seems to find in
a conversational mood.

"I can't leave the subject of the war yet.
The poor success in recruiting, and the appar-
ent apathy of the North to the fate of the
army, had filled us with disgust, and even
harder feelings. But the new order for men,
and *immediate* action by drafting, cheers
every one like a great victory. Now it looks
as if something was to be done in earnest. . .
Our band is to be mustered out to-morrow,
and, this evening, is giving farewell serenades,
which interfere materially with my writing.
They are now playing 'Ever of Thee,' — a
beautiful tune, that I am willing to devote a

good share of my precious time to hearing. I call my time 'precious' because I ought to be sleeping, preparatory to early work to-morrow morning. To-morrow is the anniversary of our departure from Massachusetts. I hope to dine with General Devens, who has invited me to a dinner-party he gives in honor of the day. . . . Many thanks for Bayard Taylor's song. I remember, now, of having seen it some time ago, and thinking it very beautiful. But Morpheus conquers me. I *must* hasten to my *blanket:* I can't call it a bed. Good-night.   Yours ever,

"RICHARD."

On the 11th of August, Captain Derby (for such he may now be called, as his commission was dated Aug. 6th, 1862) again wrote from Harrison's Landing:—

"We are again under marching orders; *i. e.*, to *hold ourselves in readiness* to move at 2 o'clock this afternoon; destination not stated. We do not *always* march when we receive such orders; but the indications now are quite strong that we are going *somewhere.*

Every one is *guessing;* and the general impression is, that the whole army is going down the James River to Fortress Monroe. . . The dinner at Gen. Devens's was a *very* pleasant affair indeed. There were about twenty present; and we spent nearly four hours in social enjoyment. . . . Major Philbrick has gone home, on twenty days' leave of absence, on account of sickness. Mr. Scandlin has at last bid us 'good-by.' We shall miss him sadly. He went down the river yesterday. The weather is hotter than ever experienced before; but there is not so much sickness as when we first came here. Flies swarm on us like the plagues of Egypt. They are almost intolerable. We have to blow them out of our tents with gunpowder."

It will be seen by the above letter, that his former captain and colonel, as well as himself, had met with deserved promotion.

On the 27th, he again writes, dating "On Transport Mississippi, off Aquia Creek, Potomac River;" and says, —

" We broke up our camp at Newport News, Sunday morning, and marched down to the landing.   Monday morning, we went on board the steamer " Mississippi,"—a large, commodious boat, built to run between Boston and New Orleans.   This morning, we arrived at the mouth of Aquia Creek, and now — three P. M. — the order has just been issued to disembark.   There are three regiments on board (about twenty-three hundred men) ; and, ours being the last, we may not get off till morning.   We shall probably go direct to Fredericksburg, as there is railroad communication with that point. Our voyage has been of great benefit to us ; giving us good rest at night, and mattressed berths, and pretty good fare at table.   I expect we have got to go into rough living again ; but it won't be as bad as what we have seen. The hottest part of the season is past, and Northern Virginia is not as unhealthy as the Peninsula.   Everybody is glad to get out of that swampy desert."

Thus he looked on the bright side. A postscript says, —

" Alexandria, Va., Thursday morning. —The

first boat-load sent ashore at Aquia Creek returned with orders to proceed to Alexandria;
and here we are, lying in the stream opposite
the city. We shall probably land during the
day."

Here may this chapter fittingly close.
Long as it is, surely it has not wearied
those who have traced, with an appre-
ciative eye, the course of the young patriot; and certainly it has been long
enough to disclose, in the frank and
candid expressions of epistolary com-
munion with a beloved mother and
sister far away, that fidelity to duty,
that ability of service, and that seldom-
spoken but faithfully-acted devotion to
the cause of his country, which was ever
worn as a robe of strength and beauty
by the young volunteer.

CHAPTER VI.

ANTIETAM.

"Dulce et decorum est pro patria mori."

"There is no death: what seems so is transition.
  This life of mortal breath
Is but a suburb of the life elysian,
  Whose portals we call death."
                                LONGFELLOW.

"Sadly and wearily *we* wait
  A gleam of peace first dawning;
To *him*, from midnight clouds, burst forth
  The calm, eternal morning."
                        MRS. ARTHUR B. FULLER.

THE earthly service of the young volunteer was now almost ended. He could have said with Paul, in more than one sense, "I am now ready to be offered, and the time of my departure is at hand. I have fought a good fight;

I have finished my course; . . . . henceforth there is laid up for me a crown." Not as an Alexander, nor as a Napoleon, had he fought, — with the lust of conquest in his soul; but as a William Tell or a Henry Havelock, — with his young, ardent, hopeful spirit stirred with the dear love of liberty, and cheered by the pure faith of the Christian. Constitutionally reticent in the expression of religious emotion or patriotic fervor, he was yet ever actuated by holy principle and an unfaltering love for the "dear old flag." He was soon to seal his attachment to the Union cause with his blood.

On the very morning of the battle of Antietam, — a day which will be ever memorable in many sad hearts, many desolated homes, — his mother received a letter, from which the following extracts are made. Even as she read it, the hope of her widowhood was going forth to the conflict with returnless steps. The letter was dated "Frederick City, Md., four P.M., Sept. 13, 1862;" and he writes, —

"MY DEAR MOTHER, — We have just marched through the city, and are bivouacking in the clover-fields near by. There has been a running fight between our advance of cavalry and flying artillery all day, but several miles from us. We could see the smoke of the cannonading on the mountains across the valley as we came down into Frederick; but it has gone over to the west side now. What the rebels mean by their movements, is a mystery; and of course our movements depend upon theirs; and I cannot tell where we shall go next. There was a rumor in the regiment this morning, that our brigade would occupy the city as a sort of provost-guard; but I see no signs of it. If we do remain here, we shall make the most of it to *fit* up and *fat* up."

A few remarks in regard to a box,

which his never-forgetful friends at home had sent to him, will give a vivid idea of the state in which such boxes often reach our heroes in the camp.

"The box has come to hand at last. When I opened it, I was quite annoyed that you did not follow my directions in regard to putting in perishable articles; but, when I saw other boxes whose contents were *completely ruined*, I thought mine would do very well. The lemons were so decayed that you could hardly tell what they were; and the can of raspberry smelt like a bottle of ammonia, and had leaked out a little. It was good luck that the cover did not drop off, and spoil every thing. The little crackers were all musty: but the cake was still nice, and the sugar; but probably the tea is infected, though I have not tried it yet. One cannot send tea packed with other articles, unless you put it in air-tight packages. That which you sent before was *clove tea* when I got it. The raisins are very nice ones, and very palatable. I haven't had opportunity to try the corn-starch; but the jelly was nearly eaten at the first opening. The ginger-wine was terrible stuff. It is regular Thompsonian medicine. I had a man attacked with colic just as I opened it; and I administered a dose with beneficial effects. The reason I wrote not to send cocoa was because I had got tired of it. It seems rather heavy for hot weather; but I can make good use of two boxes, as the mornings are getting cool. The writing-case was safe and sound. I should write on it now, but it is back in the wagon. The socks will just about carry me through the season.

"More than half the boxes sent out were a mass of rottenness. Some contained *eggs!* One had some Bologna sausages soaked in ' balm of Gilead;' which was in a thin bottle next to them. They were not improved!"

In regard to a cabinet specimen which he sent home, he says, —

"That which looks like coral *is* a piece of coral; but how it came on Malvern Hill, I do not know. Some parts of the Peninsula show numerous signs of having been, at some former period, covered with salt water. Whether that was formed on the spot, or carted on in sea-weed or guano, some geologist must determine. I saw several other similar pieces.

" I am happy to hear good news from Henry Holden. I had not seen the first report contradicted. I haven't time to-night to speak about the prospects of the war and the country. . . . Walter is urging me to come to our bread and milk, and I must close."

It is fitting that mention should here be made of the young compatriot just mentioned by Captain Derby. The first report to which he refers was doubtless in regard to his death, and was correct; for he passed to his eternal reward ten days previous to the date of Captain Derby's letter. The Rev. Edward P. Thwing, his mother's pastor, preached in Quincy, Mass., his funeral sermon on the 5th October, 1862. An extract from it is appropriately placed upon pages devoted to the memory of his friend. " They were lovely and pleasant in their lives, and in death they were not " long " divided." The following is the eloquent tribute of the Rev. Mr. Thwing to the memory of the friend and fellow-soldier of Captain Derby: —

"Among the earliest of those who left us to serve their native land was HENRY AUGUSTUS HOLDEN. Hardly nineteen years of age, with the noble spirit of self-sacrifice which the present struggle has so widely developed, he broke away from a circle of which he was the idolized centre, and voluntarily assumed the hardships of a soldier's life, far from the home which he so fondly loved. Although, still earlier in life, he had known something of absence from his native place, his heart only the fonder clung to this spot, — to brother and sister, and, above all, to the widowed mother in whose affectionate confidence he had always so largely shared. The dying injunction of his sainted father, 'Try to make her happy,' had been a law of his life, and helps to explain the filial fidelity which so eminently characterized him. The traits of mind and of heart which endeared our friend to all who knew him at home, won for him, in a remarkable degree, the affections of his comrades of the 13th. I have before me the brief but touching testimony of his chaplain, in reference to the universal esteem with which our departed friend was regarded. 'We have lost a much-loved comrade, whose memory we shall long cherish. I knew Henry well. *I have no recollection of an unworthy act in all his soldier life.*' Alluding to the fact that he died on the battle-field, he says, 'It was best for him to die thus, there on the field of *his* honor and ours; for it is by just such noble and brave boys as Henry represents, that our army and country are most distinguished.' He adds, that ' his death was perfectly peaceful, and without anguish of mind or body.' When the fatal ball entered, and he fell to the earth, he said to those about him, '*Tell my friends that I die in defence of my country.*' He lingered till Wednesday, September 3 ; when, as we trust, ' he fell asleep in Jesus,' and went to rejoin loved ones above. He had made preparation for death while in health, and hence was tranquil and serene when he drew near the confines of eternity."

Captain Derby saw the sun rise for the last time on the morning of the 17th of September, 1862. He rose as early as half-past two on that morning; and, while the breakfast was in preparation, he penned his last letter to his precious mother. It was brief; and was, *verbatim*, as follows: —

"SEPT. 17, 1862.

"MY DEAR MOTHER, — We marched from Frederick the next morning after I wrote you; and we are now encamped near Boonsborough, between that and the Potomac.

"There has been some fighting; but *we* were not engaged. It looks now as though there would be a battle before Jackson can get across the river on his retreat.

"This is a beautiful country, and we have fared quite comfortably. Weather looks rainy now; but we have shelter tents with us.

"We have very bad news from Harper's Ferry, but get no reliable particulars; yet prospects are bright with us for giving the *rebs* a good whipping at this point.

"With best love to all, I remain your affectionate son,

"RICHARD."

Three days after his heroic death, this letter reached the hands of his mother. There were to be no more letters for her from that dear, only son. Several months after, she wrote thus to a friend: "We miss so much his letters that always came so promptly. I cannot become accustomed to their absence; and am still often restless, as if watching for them." This last letter arrived at its destination on the morning after the dreadful news of his death had reached his mother's home and filled it with sadness. Yet one may well believe it was most welcome.

The battle of Antietam was that in which Captain Derby lost his life. It is now an historic event; and it may be well to speak of it at some length, before referring farther to the young patriot's part in it. The "American An-

nual Cyclopædia" for 1862 thus describes it:—

"General Burnside's corps on the left was
ordered, early in the day, to carry the bridge
across the Antietam at Rohrback's Farm, and
to attack the enemy's right. The approaches
to the bridge being in the nature of a defile,
and being swept by batteries of the enemy,
the opposite bank of the Antietam was only
reached after a severe struggle. It was afternoon before the heights were in his possession.
The enemy were driven back, and a portion
of their line was in disorder. By the most
desperate efforts, however, the enemy rallied
their retreating regiments, strengthened their
line with all their available fresh troops, and
opened batteries on the hills, from positions
which the amphitheatrical character of the
ground, it seems, abundantly furnished. General Burnside could not maintain his advantage; and was obliged to withdraw from the
extreme position he had gained near Sharpsburg, to one slightly in rear of it. He, however, held his bank of the river completely,
and maintained much ground beyond it which
he had taken from the enemy. During the

advance on the left, General Rodman was wounded. The Federal artillery is represented to have played an important part during the battle. Notwithstanding substantial and decided successes of the day, the Federal forces had suffered so severely during the conflict,—having lost 11,426 in killed and wounded, and among them many general and superior officers,—that it was deemed prudent by General McClellan to re-organize, and give rest and refreshment to the troops, before renewing the attack."

Further than this need not be quoted; for, long before General McClellan gave the order to rest, the heroic Derby had found the eternal calm.

But the graphic description by " Carleton,"* in the " Boston Journal," ought not to be omitted. He says,—

" A great battle has been fought near this village; and I sit down to write, so far as I

* Charles C. Coffin, Esq., author of " My Days and Nights on the Battle-field."

may be able, an intelligible account of the contest, — the mightiest ever fought on the continent of America. Other correspondents have doubtless anticipated me with their descriptions; but if Waterloo, after the lapse of half a century, is still studied, certainly the field of Sharpsburg or Antietam will bear one day's contemplation, now that I am able to review the field from the enemy's side. . . . The South Mountain is the easterly ridge of the Blue-Ridge chain. The Potomac cuts it at Harper's Ferry. It runs north to the vicinity of Gettysburg. Directly west of it, commencing at the Ferry, is Elk Ridge; which is about ten miles long. The village of Keitsville lies at the northern extremity of the ridge. It is a wooded elevation, eight hundred or one thousand feet high. The valley between the South Mountain and Elk Ridge is called Pleasant Valley. An unfrequented road runs over Elk Ridge. The Sharpsburg, Hagerstown, and Harper's-Ferry Turnpike runs west of the ridge, between it and the Potomac. The country along the turnpike is excellent farming-land, and has been under culture many years. It would be called an open country, — more fields than forests, —

fields, pastures with oak-groves, farm-houses, barns, wheat-stacks, corn-fields, peach and apple orchards. . . . Antietam River, which rises near Gettysburg, Penn., runs nearly south, along the western slope of Elk Ridge. Walking south-east, we find that we are gradually crossing the ridge; that there is a slope east toward the Antietam, and a gentle slope, with hills, knolls, and ravines, west toward the Potomac; that the turnpike is on the high ground between the two streams. A short distance through a beautiful oak-grove, and we come to a large ploughed field. The grove extends along the turnpike half a mile. East of the ploughed field is another grove, — the distance between the two groves a half-mile. Continuing our walk, we find the slope more abrupt as we gradually near the lower stone bridge. The eastern slope is bare of trees, but mottled with corn-fields, — the stalks beginning to wear the russet hues of autumn. There are a few farm-houses with whitewashed out-buildings. Numerous fences, smooth fields, a few apple-orchards, and a burial-ground with white head-stones, stand in pleasant contrast against the green-sward. Looking east, we have the valley of the Antietam, — this winding stream, sparkling in the sunlight, fringed with willows."

"Carleton" was nine miles off when the battle began, and rode hastily thither.

"In the first ambulance I met," he continues, "I descried a silver star, and was sorry to see, as I scrutinized the countenance, that it was my old friend Gen. Richardson, with whom I had my first experience of battle-scenes at Blackburnford. A bullet had pierced his breast.

"Several farm-houses in the vicinity were already filled with the wounded, and a long line of men with stretchers were bringing other hundreds. As fast as they were brought from the field, straw was littered upon the ground, and the sufferers laid in rows, waiting for their turn at the surgeons' hands. Here was Lieut.-Col. Dwight of the 2d Mass., Gen. Mansfield, Gen. Hooker, Gen. Sedgwick, Gen. Ricketts. There had been a terrific fire. It had rolled like the breakers on the beach, like angry thunder in the clouds, — the low, continuous growl you sometimes hear, — like

the fall of a great building: not like the
voice of many waters; for that is deep, solemn, peaceful, — the symbol of the song of the
redeemed, which will ascend before the throne
of God, when all war shall have ceased, and
all its wild uproar shall be hushed.

"Strange, mysterious Providence! that
through blood, through carnage and deso-
lation, we arrive at redemption! A year's
experience, a year's insight, has not reconciled
me to such scenes. I can accept only the
stern necessity."

"Carleton" states that Capt. Derby's
regiment, the 15th Mass., were in Gorman's brigade; as were also the 1st
Maine, and the 34th and 82d New-
York. He then continues:—

"Our troops came in front of the road;
when up rose the first rebel line. The fence
became a line of flame and smoke. The corn-
field beyond, on higher ground, was a sheet of
fire. Meagher's line, and Weber's, melted like
lead in a crucible: there Ireland bled for her
adopted home; there Delaware poured out

loyal blood; there Maryland proved her love for the grand old stars and stripes; there Richardson's veterans fought as they had fought before. With a wild rush and cheer, they moved up to the fence, ploughed through and through by the batteries above, cut and gashed by the leaden hail, and poured their volleys into the rebel ranks,—thrusting the muzzles of their guns into the enemy's faces through the fence. Then and there, they proved that they were a match for the enemy in the open field.

"The first rebel line was almost annihilated; and the dead, lying beneath the tasselled corn, were almost as numerous as the golden ears upon the stalks. Visiting the spot when the contest was over, I judged, from a little counting, that a thousand of the enemy's dead were in the road and the adjoining corn-field. A shell had thrown seven into one heap,—some on their faces, some on their backs, fallen as a handful of straws would fall when dropped upon the ground. But not they alone suffered. The bloody tide which had surged through all the morning, between the ridges above along the right, had flowed over the hill at this noontide hour. The yellow soil became crimson. The russet corn-leaves turned to red, as if autumn had put on, in a moment, its richest glory. How costly! Five thousand — I think I do not exaggerate — wounded and dead lay along that pathway and in the adjoining fields! The gods of the ancients drank human blood; but no richer libation was ever poured more willingly, freely, or bravely, than this on the heights of Sharpsburg."

The close of the contest he thus describes: —

"The day was waning. Through the hours from early morning, the war had been unceasing. Four hundred cannons had shaken the earth. Two hundred thousand men had struggled for the mastery. At times the storm had lulled, dying away like the wind at night, then rising again to the fierceness of a tornado. It was evident, by mid-afternoon, that the contest was likely to be undecisive. . . . Both parties have put on new vigor at the sunset hour. The fire kindles along the line. There is almost an unobstructed view. Far upon the right is the smoke of the thirty cannon, still rising in a white sulphurous cloud. The woods opposite, where the rebel batteries have been stationed, smoke like a furnace. A little nearer, Sumne.'s artillery is rolling its thunder and hurling its bolts against the limestone ledges; which answer, that Franklin is fresh. Ayer's battery is pouring a rapid, deadly fire on the corn-field, where the rebel line is lying under cover. Above them, on the highest hillock, a half-mile from Sharpsburg, a heavy rebel battery is in flame. Richardson's artillery, immediately in front, is replying, sending shells upon the hill, and beyond into Sharpsburg, where hay-stacks, houses, and barns are burning, rolling up tall pillars of cloud and flame to heaven. At our left hand, Burnside's heavy guns are thundering, answered by the opposing batteries. All the country is smoking, as if the last great day had come, and lightning was leaping from the earth. It is a continuous roll of thunder. The sun goes down reddened in the smoky haze. Ayer's battery is directly in line with the descending orb; and the sharp, swift flashes seem to issue from its angry face. The musketry has ceased, save a few volleys rolling from beyond the willows in the valley, and a little dripping, like rain-drops after a shower, in front and on the right, where the skirmishers are in line. Words utterly fail to convey an idea of the grandeur of the scene. It has passed from sight; but it will remain in memory one of the grandest pictures of the war.

" The thunder died away, the flashes became few and fainter, ceased, and all was still upon the bloody field. Thirty thousand, full of life at the dawning, were bleeding at this evening hour. The sky was bright with the lurid flames of the burning buildings; and they who went out with a cup of cold water to the wounded, needed no torch to light them on their errands of mercy. A thousand camp-fires gleamed along the hillsides, as if a great city had lighted its lamps.

" The ambulances were winding on, in the morning, over the fields. Along all the roads, supply-trains came. Troops poured in, — twenty-five thousand men ready for the renewal of the contest in the morning. Cavalry clattered along all the streets. Additional artillery came up; and the army, notwithstanding the gory harvest of the day, had full ranks for the ensuing morning. The slightly wounded

were pouring to the village of Keitsville,—
hundreds, with bandaged arms, hands, and
feet, seeking a place to lie down, in houses,
barns, or under haystacks. It was a mournful
sight. Yet there were but few complaints.
The good people, kind and Christian, opened
their houses, hands, and hearts to the sufferers.
It was cheering,—almost the only redeeming
feature of the hour. So the day closed; re-
minding one of the sweet lines of Whittier, in
the ' Angel of Buena Vista,' —

' Not wholly lost, O Father! is this evil world of ours:
  Upward, through its blood and ashes, spring afresh the
    Eden flowers!'

. . . " Such are the main features of this great
contest,— the mightiest ever fought on the
continent; in which it is believed that twenty-
five to thirty thousand men have fallen. It is
a battle-field which will be much visited and
studied. Lee's intentions, his plans, his positions, will be inquired into and criticised in
years to come; and so the battle, as fought by
General McClellan, will be studied by those
who admire and those who do not accept him
as a great general.

" It is b it a faint outline I have given of one

of the sublimest battle-fields the world ever saw; indecisive, apparently, of present issue; but, for aught we know, a great turning-point in history!"

Captain Derby was spared the anguish he must have felt, had he lived through all the carnage of that dreadful day; for he was among those first called to lay down their lives for their country. His companion and friend, Lieutenant (now Captain) Gale, thus described his last hours in a letter to the bereaved mother, dated Bolivar, Va., Sept. 24, 1862: —

"My DEAR MADAM, — I trust that you will pardon my delay in giving you the particulars of that sad event, the announcement of which must have already reached you. Our poor wounded comrades have engrossed so much of our attention, that we have not found time to communicate with the friends and relatives of those gone from us to return no more. Even now, it is painful, in the extreme, to bring up again the picture of that terrible day.

"We left camp in cheerful spirits, though with something like a premonition that great events were at hand. I chatted pleasantly with Richard, who was almost a brother to me; and we went forward hand in hand, as it were, as we had often done before. When we approached the enemy, he asked me to attend to the men on the right of the company, while he gave orders to those on the left. In a moment, heavy volleys were poured into our ranks; and finding myself slightly wounded, I sought the shelter of a tree. While binding my wound, I saw the Lieutenant cheering on his men in the most heroic manner: it was a scene that I never can forget. Two minutes later, he also was laid at the foot of the tree, fatally wounded in the temple. He was quite unconscious, apparently in almost a childlike sleep; and thus, without suffering, he passed from life to immortality. Oh! how sadly did his dear friend Major Philbrick, and myself, gaze upon his fair face! We exchanged significant and sorrowful glances; and, looking at the battle before us, we found ourselves nearly surrounded by the enemy. Hastily retreating, we were obliged to leave our dead and wounded; but, before this, I had secured every thing of value about our dear brother except his sword and belt: this was so firmly fastened, that I could not secure it.

"On the following day, we made three attempts to get across to those who were left behind; but the enemy refused to grant this privilege. On Friday, the field was deserted; and so much time had elapsed since the engagement, that it was almost impossible to recognize the most familiar faces. Such a great change had taken place, that we were obliged to relinquish our desire to send home the remains for interment; and they were buried in a small garden-spot, quite near the scene of action. It is known as the Lucca Place, and is about one mile from the village of Sharpsburg. Any one in the neigborhood will point out the location, — the exact spot is marked by a head-board, — and the proprietor has promised that this, together with those that are near it, shall be preserved.

"Yesterday, Major Philbrick and myself, with the aid of a borrowed key (his own being lost), unlocked his valise, and placed in it his watch, pistol, gold ring, and other articles of value. To-day, I have directed this to you at Auburndale, and shall forward it by Adams' Express;

and, if I can be of any farther service, do not, I beg of you, fail to allow me the privilege.

"I had found him such a genial companion, with so much to love and respect, that I could not quite reconcile myself to the thought that we were parted for this life; and yet I almost longed to be with him, if I might leave such a fair name and glorious record. This line is constantly in my mind, and will always associate itself with his memory : —

' That life is long which answers Life's great end.'

"Deeply sympathizing with you in your great bereavement,

"I am, with much respect,

"Your obedient servant,

"WALTER GALE."

Other testimonies than the above letter came to the mother at various times, showing in what high estimation her son was held. Colonel W. Raymond Lee wrote thus : —

"Your son, during the short time of his

connection with my regiment, endeared himself very much to our regard and respect. While glad of his promotion on his own account, we regretted our loss.

"Duty brought me personally in contact with him on the evening of Oct. 20. On Oct. 21, I again met him on the field. His deportment was most creditable to a gentleman of his traditions."

Major James H. Rice, of the 19th Massachusetts Regiment, whom Captain Derby met in the Peninsula campaign, where they were on picket duty together, writes, —

"My associations with your lamented and noble son were of a most pleasant nature, and not at all times devoid of peril; and on that account his remembrance is to me a source of pride and pleasure. I will not seek again to open those wounds which you, his mother, must feel at his early death : but will only say, that, as his life had been pure, so his death was glorious ; and he was one of those of whom I can truly say, —

'He should have died hereafter.'"

His friend and counsellor, J. L. Andrews, Esq., wrote an obituary notice of Captain Derby; in which occur these words : —

"Lieutenant Derby combined courage and patriotism with the polish of a gentleman, and the most prepossessing manners and form. He was rising rapidly in the army; and his death is a severe loss to his kindred, his many friends, and to the country."

His former teacher, Rev. Dr. Allen, wrote to the "Northborough Times" as follows : —

"Among the killed of the great battle of Wednesday, Sept. 17, was Richard Derby, 1st Lieutenant of Co. C, of the 15th Regiment. As his name in the first reports was misspelled, and the name of the regiment not rightly given, we hoped, and even against hope, that he was yet spared for other service and future usefulness. But our worst fears are confirmed. . . . He was a beautiful, gentle, sweet-tempered, yet manly boy; the idol of his mother and sister, and a universal favorite. He was endeared to us by a residence in our family, in the capacity of a pupil, when a lad; from which time our interest in him has never ceased or declined. . . . He was a favorite, as we learn, with the officers and privates of his company and regiment; and we were pleased to hear from his colonel (now General Devens) so good an account as he gave us of our favorite pupil, — one whom we had loved and cherished almost as one of our own children."

Chaplain Fuller, in a letter to the bereaved mother, wrote, —

"My whole heart sympathizes with you in your affliction. From his childhood up to the hour of his death, I loved your Richard as if one of my own family. He was a noble, pure, and saintly young man; and his death was as heroic and honorable as his whole life had been worthy. Fitting close to a most excellent career! I saw him in the army; and there he was loved and respected by all. Little did I think, in pressing his hand in parting at Harrison's Landing, that it was for the last time. My tears mingle with those of his kindred; for I, too, have lost in him a friend, loved as a younger brother. And yet not *lost:* for heaven is composed of such as *he;* and we must live faithful to duty and to God, that *there* we may meet *him* and our other loved friends. My most sympathizing remembrance to your daughter and family.

"Most truly your friend,

"A. B. FULLER."

Only ten months after this letter was penned, the writer was killed at Fredericksburg, and went up to join his friend, where no sound of war is ever heard.

Rev. N. G. Allen wrote from Somerville, Mass., to Mrs. Derby, —

"It was with deep sadness, and heartfelt condolence for his afflicted family, that I read the record of your son's death. Ever since his departure to the seat of war, we have both experienced much anxious solicitude for his fortunes amid the perils of battle. Nor did a little of that solicitude arise from a sense of the great loss and void his death would occasion to your mother-loving heart, and to his sister and her children. For himself, I was not so anxious; for I believed him to be a thoughtful young man, — conscientious, moral, and upright, and likewise religious. . . . I had great sympathy and respect for his style of mind and character. Meek, unobtrusive, reflecting, and elevated, he was singularly decided, and entirely self-possessed. His commendable and ingenuous devotion to his family makes his patriotism of a very high order ; because he could forego, as it were, so readily and so promptly, the charms of domestic bliss and the strong ties of kin for the earnest call which his country made upon her loyal sons. As the memory of his affection and kind acts for his own will never fade from their hearts, so his name will ever after be mentioned with tenderness and respect by his few surviving comrades, and many others who have heard of his rare worth and true bravery. Nor is it too much to say of him what is spoken, by the poet-laureate, of England's greatest and now departed general, —

> ' Whatever record springs to light,
> *He never shall be shamed.*'

"And now, my dear madam, let me point you to Him who doeth all things *well*, as the only adequate support in the calamities of life. ' Cast thy burden upon the Lord, and he shall sustain thee.' " . . .

The following letter, from one of Capt. Derby's dearest friends, should have a place here : —

"So. DANVERS, MASS., Oct. 11, 1862.

"MY DEAR MRS. DERBY,—I received from Rebecca, this morning, the lock of dear Richard's hair, which you were so kind as to send me. It is a gift which I prize very, very highly; and for which I beg of you to accept my heartfelt thanks. It will serve, in coming time, to remind me, though I shall not need it for that, of my fortunate acquaintance with one whom I can only think of with love and admiration. Richard came nearer to my ideal of true manhood than any friend I have ; and, in losing him, I feel that I have lost a golden link from the chain which makes life desirable, and have gained new incentive for so employing life, that, when my day of departure comes, I shall be able to regain the golden link, and enjoy more truly his noble worth.

"We need not mourn that Richard is gone, so much as that we, too, are not prepared to tread in his steps.

"For him we cannot mourn; but for ourselves, for our country, and for humanity's sake, we cannot easily dry our tears. Yet we know, that we, that our country and humanity, are in the hands of a just and wise God, who does nothing amiss. And ought we not to submit with cheerfulness to his ruling? It is want of faith in the eternal right, and in our future re-union, which makes our grief so hard to bear. The more we trust, the more we are prepared to suffer and to do. Let us then, bearing in mind Richard's excellence, cherish and emulate his virtues! Again thanking you for your kind remembrance of me, I subscribe myself

"Yours very respectfully,

"D. WEBSTER KING."

One more letter must be mentioned. It is from Capt. Derby's earliest friend: they were like David and Jonathan.

"TROY, N. Y., Sept. 28, 1862.

"MRS. M. A. DERBY, and others most nearly related to Richard.

"AFFLICTED FRIENDS, — It was with a sorrow that must return at many a future hou' as times and places shall remind me of it, that I learned, from a home-letter of Friday last, of the undoubted death in battle of your dear son, and my long-cherished and always more and more esteemed friend Richard. . . . For seventeen long years, I knew and loved him. I remember him (and this may interest the children, his thoughtfully loved nephew and nieces) when but eleven years old, a daily morning visitor at father's door on his little errand of domestic duty, then my desk-fellow at school, often my bedfellow and table-companion, and everywhere my cherished playmate. How his little self, in old times, fancied my strength to be great! while I felt as a sort of champion for him. He once threw his arms around my neck, in the little cottage which I shall henceforth, more than ever, behold with recollections of him oppressively serious, and told me I seemed to him more like a father than a brother. I did labor most successfully in establishing him in all healthful habits; and though the best are but bungling apprentices in handling Christ's holy religion, yet I hope, that, amid much error of method in trying to share religious blessings with him, some good influences may have been felt by him from me.

" What now is the magnitude of the crime of rebellion, which causes the sacrifice of such lives! and what the appalling crime against human souls, out of which such rebellion grew! We must regard God, not as an unconcerned but a most interested spectator of the present war; and not as a spectator only, but an almighty and all-righteous actor, whose terrible decisions we must willingly submit ourselves as instruments to execute. With the intelligent understanding of the cause which Richard had, he could not but have laid down his precious life as a pious sacrifice; and as we contemplate this, and his simple sincerity and single-mindedness, his tender care of the heart-life of the children, and that touching request of his for a prayer-book for use with dying prisoners, let us think of his unfettered spirit breaking through the murky war-cloud, and welcomed by a shining host with notes not heard by mortal ear: and, thinking of all this, may not the livelier heartstring which his death broke be replaced by one whose mellower note of comforted sorrow shall never be silent to the ear of hope and faith in a Saviour's *divine compassion* and *great salvation?*

"Respectfully and sincerely yours,

"S. EDWARD WARREN."

It will be remembered that the valise of the young patriot was sent home. In it was found a letter, so preserved as to show it was highly prized, from one of those Salem cousins with whom Capt. Derby spent many happy days in boyhood. It was dated Nov. 9, 1861; and the following extracts will be read with interest, both on account of the friendly regard manifested for the young patriot, and for the mention of one, at least, who has gained historic renown and a hero's grave. The letter commences,—

"MY DEAR RICHARD,—You may feel **very**

sure, that, with anxious hearts and eager eyes, we searched all the newspaper accounts for tidings of our little soldier boy; and rejoiced to find the familiar *family name* was not to be seen among the mournful record of 'dead, wounded, missing, or prisoner.' We felt the rank to which you had attained would have caused distinct mention to have been made of you, if any thing disastrous had happened; and so we tried hard to believe all was well with you: yet we did rejoice to receive confirmation of your safety, in a letter from your uncle George,* who very kindly wrote me of your narrow escape from drowning, and your rescue by Col. Devens. . . . We rejoice to find you suffered no injury more severe than exhaustion. How little we thought (as you made your first acquaintance with sea-bathing under our auspices) that the feeble little boy whom we encouraged in his first experiments of swimming would come so near losing his life by the treacherous element, in gallant defence of his country! Yesterday, my mother had the honor and pleasure of receiving a letter from Gen. Lander (written

* Surgeon Derby, of 23d Massachusetts Regiment.

13

sitting up in bed), to inform us 'that Lieut. Derby is safe. I telegraphed,' he writes, ' to know if he was dead, wounded, or missing; and enclose the general's answer, which I am proud and happy to copy for you:—

" From POOLESVILLE, to Brig.-Gen. Lander.

"Lieut. Derby is alive, and adjutant of the regiment, vice Hicks, promoted.—Signed, C. P. Stone, B. G."

" ' Had you been informed of your promotion when you wrote me? or was it your modesty alone prevented your telling us the welcome news? We sincerely congratulate you upon this reward of your valor and patriotism; but do not let it incite you to run into any unnecessary dangers in your military ardor. I knew you must be gratified to learn you were an object of interest to those who take such high position in this fearful struggle.' . . . We have been quite busy knitting army socks. I should hope some of them would reach you; but the pattern was so preposterously large, that I fear they would prove a terrible clog, and absorb a vast quantity of water, supposing you should again be doomed to another swimming match. I can only reiterate our warmest wishes for your health and safety, and beg you not to incur any unnecessary dangers."

Capt. Derby was a member of the Masonic order, having joined Revere Lodge in Boston. By his "brethren of the mystic tie" he is mourned as one who recommended the principles of Masonry by a life conformed to the compass and the square.

Thus it may be seen, that the young patriot was the object of loving interest to many warm and noble hearts, from the dawn of his life at Medfield to its sanguinary close at Antietam.

CHAPTER VII.

DUST TO DUST.

" Thou bad'st this soldier son of thine
    Go forth in armor bright:
He fell, as Israel's beauty fell,
    Upon the mountain height.

Give him a grave among the hills
    That knew his boyhood's tread;
And in those green-roofed aisles repeat
    The service for the dead."

MARY WEBB.

Y dint of great perseverance and untiring effort, the remains of Captain Derby were recovered, through the efficient services of his friend and cousin, George S. Derby, Esq., of Boston; and although on their arrival East no one was able to behold them, yet it was a source of great satisfaction to his friends and family, that they could be laid to rest beside those of his father in the family burial-place.

Services were first held at his mother's residence in Auburndale, Mass., — a rural village in the town of Newton, some ten miles from Boston, in Middlesex County, and on the line of the Worcester Railroad.

These services were designed to be comparatively private; but so great was the interest of the neighbors in the dear young man when living, and so interested were all patriotic hearts in regard to the fact that he died for his country, that there was a large gathering of sympathizing friends. Eloquent and appropriate remarks were made by Rev. Washington Gilbert, the Unitarian clergyman of West Newton; and a fervent, heart-

breathed prayer was offered by the Rev.
E. W. Clark, formerly the Congregational
clergyman of Auburndale, and afterward
chaplain in the 47th Massachusetts Regiment. The services closed with the singing of a hymn, accompanied by music
from the piano, which Captain Derby had
often loved to hear. The funeral procession was then formed; and loving, mourning friends followed the dear remains to
the quiet spot in Medfield which he had
himself caused to be adorned as the family resting-place.

The beautiful church where his parents
were long accustomed to worship, and
whose aisles his own infant feet had trod,
was decorated to receive him. Like a
crowned conqueror, he passed within
those open doors; and starry flags and
beautiful flowers told that one came
whom the free people of a struggling

nation delighted to honor. But the Angel of Death passed in at his side ; and so there were tears instead of plaudits, and subdued voices of sympathy and sorrow rather than the huzzas of victory and the shouts of rejoicing.

Old friends threw open the doors of their hospitable mansions for the reception of those who came to bury the departed hero; and, ere the funeral *cortége* entered the village, it was met by a procession of those who knew the sainted soldier in "days agone," and were desirous to pay every tribute of respect to his precious memory.

A band of music accompanied the procession; and the thrilling tones of martial instruments, sounding out a funeral dirge for a warrior slain, went forth sweetly and sadly on the autumnal air. Some in the procession bore garlands and

wreaths of appropriate flowers to deck
the bier of the early dead, as if their
hearts had responded to the words of
Mrs. Hemans, —

" Bring flowers, pale flowers, o'er the bier to shed, —
  A crown for the brow of the early dead !
  For this through its leaves hath the white rose burst;
  For this in the woods was the violet nursed.
  Though they smile in vain for what once was ours,
  They are Love's last gift: bring ye flowers, pale flow-
      ers."

They proceeded to the church : and
there the services were conducted by
Captain Derby's former teacher, Rev. Dr.
Joseph Allen ; Rev. C. W. Sewall, of Medfield ; and Rev. Arthur B. Fuller, chaplain
of the 16th Regiment, — then at home
on a furlough because of sickness. Every
word of prayer and address and hymn
was appropriate, and grateful to the
hearts of the mourning household band;

but the bereaved mother has often regretted that no "reporter" was present
to catch the words as they fell from the
lips of the several speakers. As she
remarked, in the unreserve of friendly
correspondence, "Every word of Arthur's
was like inspiration, and ought to have
been written in letters of gold." Chaplain Fuller's own heart, we know, was on
fire for liberty and the right; and his
devotion to his country led him fully to
appreciate and honor the character of
the brave young hero who was lying in
the death-slumber before him. He had,
as has been shown, met with the young
patriot, not long before, amid the scenes
of strife; and, in his own eloquent manner, he referred to that meeting, described
the delicate-looking young man moving
gently about among the sick and wounded, himself so feeble as to need support,

yet always with a kind word, or perhaps
even more,—with some delicacy designed
for himself, sharing it with a less-favored
comrade; and left the impression on all
hearts that the example of the noble
dead was enough to stimulate the companions of his boyish days to patriotic
exertions, and to make every man anxious to " do something for his country."

During the interesting services, the following hymn was sung. It is from the
pen of William B. Fowle, a well-known
teacher and author, whose home is now
in Medfield.

> We lay this offering on thine altar,
>   God of Freedom, God of Right:
> This young heart was not born to falter
>   In Humanity's great fight.
>
> We may not sorrow for him stricken;
>   Liberty's great price is life;
> And seeds like this shall, dying, quicken
>   Many a hero for the strife.

Our solemn sacrifice is wending
    Like sweet perfume to the sky.
Patriot spirits, now ascending,
    Bid us dare, like him, to die, —

Die, to seal a life of glory ;
    Die, to gain a holy fame ;
Die, to crush foul Treason's fury ;
    Die, when still to live were shame.

Long life consists not in the number
    Of our years of pilgrimage :
Length of days may life encumber;
    " Youth unspotted is old age."

When the services beneath the consecrated roof were concluded, they passed
out into God's great temple, whose " arch
is the unmeasured sky;" and slowly,
with reversed arms and muffled drum,
they bore him to the grave.   There a
touching scene occurred, which brought
tears to many sunburnt faces : and eyes
all unused to weep were speedily dimmed,

as a fair young girl, supported by her brother, stepped forth to the star-spangled coffin of the heroic dead, with a basket of fragrant flowers in her hand; which she took quietly, one by one, kissed them, and then dropped them gently on the coffin, — affection's last offering to one who loved flowers, and ever looked on them as —

> "Emblems of our own great resurrection,
> Emblems of the bright and better land."

The usual volley was not fired at the grave; as the bereaved friends felt that it would too vividly recall the battle-scenes which had deprived them of one so dear.

The solemn funeral services were at an end ; and the noble form was left in that quiet spot, while the mourners turned tearfully away.

> "He sleeps his last sleep, he has fought his last battle :
> No sound can awake him to glory again."

Oh, how many in our land have learned, as they never learned before, the force of Mrs. Heman's description ! —

> " By the drum's dull, muffled sound ;
>   By the arms that sweep the ground ;
>   By the volleying musket's tone, —
>   Speak ye of a soldier gone
>   In his manhood's pride."

This brave soldier's loved ones turned away from that precious grave, and passed on to a home rendered desolate by the hand of war.

And yet they were comforted. They had laid their loved one down, as one who was — to use the language of the church he loved — " in the testimony of a good conscience ; in the confidence of a certain faith ; in the comfort of a reasonable, religious, and holy hope ; in favor with God ; and in perfect charity with all the world." *

---

* " Book of Common Prayer,"— Office for the Visita'ion of the Sick.

They did not doubt, for one moment, the comforting doctrine of immortality.

How the stricken mother felt in that sad hour may be learned from her own words : —

"We committed all that was mortal of our dear one to the earth by the side of his father; and that spot, 'the grave of so many hopes, around which so many dear memories gather, shall also be the birthplace of affections and desires infinitely more precious.' The curtain has fallen, and all is dark. And yet not so; for, although I cannot now penetrate the gloom, I know that there is light beyond, and it will re-appear."

There was one in that sorrowing band, the cherished friend of the bereaved mother and sister, who would have claimed a dearer title had the hero lived to return from the war. She it was who made the last offering of flowers at his burial. To her, Capt. Derby had been attached from boyhood; and, as his mother states, "they were every way worthy of each other. She now mourns his early departure, and feels that she gave to her country's need a most precious sacrifice." At the request of Capt. Derby's mother, the following lines were penned for her by the writer of this memorial: —

THE SOLDIER'S BETROTHED.

Stricken, bereaved, forlorn, — a widow sad
    In all but name, —
How dark the path the lone betrothed must tread !
    The scroll of Fame
Bearing meanwhile the name most dear to her,
    As one who fell
In Freedom's strife, a holy conqueror,
    Who hath fought well!

One light alone her pathway now can gild, —
    That from above ;
Where the dear voice, on earth forever stilled,
    Chanteth, in love,

High praises by the throne of the Eternal,
    That ne'er shall end.
Oh! in the heavenly season soft and vernal,
    Their songs shall blend !

Those parted lovers yet again shall meet,
    When o'er the wave
She passes to that shore with willing feet,
    And finds the grave
The gate of joy her spirit never knew
    On this side heaven ;
While a blest union with the brave and true
    Henceforth is given.

O loving Saviour ! once in human form,
    Sustain thy child, —
The stricken one, who lonely braves the storm,
    Though dark and wild ;
Help her upon thy mighty arm to lean,
    Till she shall meet
Him, from whom death her sweet love cannot wean,
    At thy dear feet !

A friend, who had known Capt. Derby from his youth,[*] wrote thus in the " Waltham Sentinel : " —

[*] J. L. Andrews, Esq.

"The past week has brought home the body of another patriot soldier, — Richard Derby, of Auburndale. He was instantly killed at the battle of Antietam, while, as lieutenant-commanding, he was gallantly leading on his company in the conflict. . . . His body now rests quietly by the side of his father in that pleasant country churchyard. His mother, a widow, weeps with thousands of other widows and mothers; so many 'Rachels weeping for their children, and will not be comforted, because they are not.' He was a young man of uncommon promise, dearly beloved by all who knew him, quiet and unobtrusive. . . . Thus another sacrifice — pure, acceptable, we trust — has been laid on the altar of Liberty. May it help to bring an honorable peace to our beloved country! — a peace founded on truth, right, and justice; the only peace worth fighting for, and which will redound to the lasting good of the whole people."

The mourners were not without sympathy. From far and near came letters of condolence. One who was a dear

14

friend to the departed, while in the far
West, wrote, in November following, —

"I should have written you long ago; but
delayed, not wishing to intrude even *my sympathies* upon the bitter grief and mourning
which you have been called upon to suffer.
Poor Richard! I cannot realize that I shall
never see *him*, my dear friend, again on earth.
I cannot think of him except as I last saw
him, so full of life and health; so anxious that
I, his Western friend, should enjoy myself
when with him; so beloved by every one, — an
embodiment of all that was *good* and *noble*
and *manly*. I loved him as I would a brother;
and the death of any brother of mine would
not cause me more bitter grief. Alas for us
all, that God, in his inscrutable providence,
should see fit to take such an one from us!
but, my dear friend, we know this, that 'he
doeth all things well.' We must bow before such
bitter strokes, with the prayer, 'Thy will, not
mine, be done.' And then the parting is not
long. We all shall soon be crossing the river.
No more mourning then, — no partings; but
an everlasting enjoyment of the society of those

we love, if we live and die loving the Father, as I believe our dear Richard did."

The patriotic mother of the young hero, herself, wrote, after the battle of Gettysburg, — which occurred nearly a year after her son's death, — words which prove her to have been worthy to be the mother of such a son. These are some of them : —

" Our Massachusetts boys were not mere machines, coarse and brutal stuff, ' food for powder ; ' but the best blood, the brightest hopes, the noblest, fairest young men, the flower and pride of our best homes. New England sent her best when the call, ' To arms ! ' sounded among her hills. Our brave ones have indeed ' covered themselves with honor.' Heavy losses come with our victories ; and we could scarcely bear to rejoice, did we not know that those who have fallen *now*, and *earlier* in the struggle, would ardently join us, could they speak. We have poured out, at Gettysburg, another costly libation of blood, drawn from the veins of the youth and manhood

of our land: but they felt that their country
called; and they have laid down their lives in
the holy cause, and ascended on high to join the
immortal Washington and his compatriots. As
we, bereaved mothers and sisters and friends,
sit weeping at home, counting among the killed
our dear sons and brothers, what an unuttera-
ble pang shoots through the heart! Nature
must, for the hour, have her due in sighs and
tears and choking agony. But soon the
thought comes, that they fell for their
country, and her great cause; and that their
sacrifices will bring joy and peace and freedom
to generations yet unborn. Therefore *we*
must be comforted; for our dear Richard still
lives, and is glorified. His life was not wasted
in the great struggle for his country and its
institutions. He and they have paid a costly
price for a magnificent good. They have won
the meed of eternal honor and remembrance.
We shall never be obliged to write of our dear
ones, *craven* or *coward* or *traitor*; for they
have sealed their testimony with their blood:
and we can forever unite, and sing, ' Honor to
the brave! Blessings on the loyal! Praise
from heaven and earth to the noble soldier
who was not afraid to die, so his country
should live!' "

In the beautiful cemetery of the town of Medfield, not far from the monument of the Rev. Dr. Prentiss, the venerable and excellent pastor of a church in that place for many years, is reared the elegant marble shaft which commemorates the heroic Derby. It stands upon a granite pedestal; and upon its summit is an urn surmounted by emblematic flowers. Upon the front is inscribed, —

CAPT. RICHARD C. DERBY,

FIFTEENTH REGIMENT MASSACHUSETTS VOLUNTEERS,

Fell at Antietam, Sept. 17, 1862,

Aged 28 years.

"That life is long which answers Life's great end."

On one side of the monument are inscribed the names of Captain Derby's father and of an infant brother; and, on the other, the sweet assurance of the poet, —

" There is no death: what seems so is transition."

Around the base of the monument

grows ivy, from the very plant which Captain Derby was wont to tend; and over his grave is festooned myrtle from his garden-plat at Auburndale. A noble pine and other trees adorn the spot; and beautiful flowers grow in an urn, prepared for the purpose, within the enclosure. Thus the spot where the young patriot rests is rendered, as far as possible, so tasteful in appearance, as to be in keeping with his singularly pure and symmetrical character.

CHAPTER VIII.

POETICAL TRIBUTES.

"O brave poets! keep back nothing;
  Nor mix falsehood with the whole!
Look up Godward! speak the truth in
  Worthy song from earnest soul!
Hold in high poetic duty
Truest Truth the fairest Beauty!"

MRS. BROWNING

SHORTLY after the funeral of her darling son, the sorely stricken mother, with a heart moved by Christian faith and unshaken patriotism, caused a small pamphlet to be printed, entitled "Words of Sympathy for Mothers who weep for Sons slain in Battle." This consoling memento of her beloved son the sympathizing moth-

er scattered far and wide among the bereaved mothers, now, alas! so numerous
in our land. The first poem in it was,
appropriately enough, a tribute to the
memory of her son, from the pen of Miss
Caroline Derby, of Salem, and was published at first in the columns of the "Salem Gazette."

The land is rich in beauty : the gayly smiling sod,
Like the King to Royal Esther, holds out her golden rod ;
While in her purple robes of state, with dew-drops glit-
    tering sheen,
The trembling aster sways and bends, as bowed the sup-
    pliant queen :
On the dark hill, the evergreen shoots up its church-like
    spire,
And the maple sheds its ruddy leaves like flakes of living
    fire :
Autumn's rich beauty waits us here, — but we turn away
    unmoved ;
For our thoughts are round a soldier's bier, with the
    noble boy we loved!

It seems but yesterday the boy sprang fondly to our
    arms,
All bright with childhood's radiant joy, all fair with child-
    hood's charms :

It seems but yesterday his hand was closely clasped in
    ours;
And his young feet, beside our own, were wandering
    'midst the flowers.
Still, Nature smiles in quiet grace, as in that earlier
    day;
Woodbine and violets keep their place : but *he* has passed
    away!
Still bright in beauty smile the scenes through which his
    boyhood roved;
But Death has plucked the fairest flower, — the noble boy
    we loved!

For early manhood came; and War's stern clarion sum-
    moned all:
Son of a time-proved ancestry, he answered to the call.
Those careless feet have fearless stood where fell the
    iron hail;
That baby hand has waved command where Valor's self
    might quail;
Those truthful eyes grew dim in death on Freedom's
    gory sod;
That loyal heart has kept its faith to country and to
    God;
That faith, by patriot sires bequeathed, he kept all un-
    disproved, —
And we may *weep*, but never *blush*, for the noble boy we
    loved!

When through this baptism of blood our land regenerate
    stands;
And Peace and Freedom meet once more, with closely
    clasping hands;

While, to the joy bells' loud acclaim, the rocking turrets
    reel,
And Peace, from out the cannon's lips, shall speak in
    thunderous peal;
When, with glad shouts of " Victory ! " our joyful legions
    come, —
We shall but see a *drooping* flag, and hear a *muffled*
    drum :
We would not mar the general joy, nor be our tears re-
    proved,
Who count, amid the costs of War, the noble boy we
    loved !

The following elegiac lines were written by one of America's most honored
female writers, at the request of Captain
Derby's friends, and forwarded to the bereaved mother, with expressions of heartfelt sympathy from one whose " Faded
Hope " will ever be read with tearful interest by every widowed mother who
has parted from an only son : —

" THE ONLY SON OF HIS MOTHER, AN. SHE A WIDOW."

BY MRS. L. H. SIGOURNEY.

O widow with the only son !
    Say, is it well with him ?

As the bright days of boyhood run,
He sports, he leaps, the stream he dares,
For no fatigue or danger cares,
   Health sparkling in his eye,
And vigor quickening every limb,
Yet gladly to the school resorts,
And reverent treads the holy courts;
And the mother answered joyously,
   " Yes : it is well with him."

O widow with the only son !
   Say, is it well with him ?
There's a wild storm-cloud in the sky, —
It darkeneth our planet's rim, —
   A cry of war from South to North.
The flag unfurls, the banners fly,
And valiantly he marches forth !
   I hear the mother sigh ;
Yet in her heart was sown of old
A patriot ardor, not grown cold :
Its zeal o'ercame her fears ;
And so she answered, through her tears,
   " Yes : it is well with him."

O mother with the only son !
   Say, is it well with him ?
There is a thundering battle-cry,
And thousands lay them down to die .
There is a sound of funeral wail,
A manly form all cold and pale ! —
   Mother, thy light is dim !
But He who once at Calvary bled,

> With piercèd side, and drooping head,
>   Saveth the soul that clings to Him:
> He, whose strong arm hath conquered Death,
> In his unbounded mercy saith,
>   " Yes: it is well with him."

The author of that popular song, " Do they miss me at Home?" with many other rhythmical expressions of true and noble sentiment, thus responded to a request for a tribute to the young patriot's memory: —

CAPT. RICHARD C. DERBY.

BY MRS. CAROLINE A. MASON.

So young to die! but there are lives whose sun
Goes down in glory ere the day is done;
And such was his.   O rare and royal soul!
In Life's young morning reaching Life's great goal,
And laying down his armor, with the prize
Waiting the gaze of his expiring eyes!
Say no dark requiem o'er his early grave:
, Weep human tears! yo *must!* the life he gave
For hearth and home, and native land, was dear,
And Love will have its way above his bier, —
But let no murmur mingle with your grief:
His life, so brave, so beautiful, so brief,
Has borne its blossoms, — lay it calm away:
Its fruit shall ripen in eternal day!

Oh ! if there be one grave above the rest
Revered and honored, beautified and blest,
'Tis where a CHRISTIAN PATRIOT makes his rest !
There shall the bright sun shed its earliest gleams,
There linger longest in his parting beams :
There troops of happy birds, on sportive wing,
" Trill their sweet descants" in the early spring :
There wintry snows fall purest : Summer there
Wave her first blossoms and her balmiest air ;
And Autumn bring its wealth of golden bloom
And crimson leaves to decorate the tomb ;
And grateful, loving hearts, o'erplant the spot
With shining laurel and forget-me-not :
There Love resort, to smile as well as weep ;
Saying, " 'Tis well ! his memory we will keep ;
'Tis well ! ' He giveth His beloved sleep ! ' "

THE FRUITS OF WAR.

BY MABELLE.

" The greatest glory of these times, even of this war,
lies not in the triumph of battle-fields; not in the splendid successes of our military skill ; not even the saving of
our Nation's life : but it lies in the noble qualities of
manhood that the time has called forth; in the capacity
for endurance and uncomplaining suffering that is everywhere displayed." — Extract from a letter by Mrs. M. A.
Derby, Auburndale, Mass.

How true, poor mother, are those words
Wrung from thine anguished soul,

While watching him, thy sainted child,
    Whose feet have reached the goal!
With joy we follow him, and scan
The noblest work of God in man!

Then mark how perfect was his life ;
    And what a glorious crown
Our nation yet will twine for him
    Whose sun, ere noon, went down !
But, when it faded from thy sight,
It left for thee no starless night.

And, when his Master called him home,
    He went, with full, ripe sheaves ;
While those who live may yet be found
    With nought but withered leaves.
The Reaper on that battle-field
Knew which the perfect fruit would yield.

And over him death had no power ;
    His work is not yet done ;
Nor should we feel a life was lost,
    That had such triumphs won !
He left a record few could claim,
While green the bays around his name.

And in the higher, holier life,
    Which all around we see,
We, trembling, hope to bear a part,
    Though humble it may be,
While waiting here the glorious dawn
That ushers in sweet Freedom's morn.

For not alone upon the field
  Are all the heroes seen :
The prayers from loving hearts at home
  Have kept those laurels green ;
And strength they needed to endure
Has come from Love's home-altar pure.

If this the fruit of these dark days,
  What must God's harvest be,
And, with these precious garnered sheaves,
  The one he took from thee ?
In this great work, brave, suffering heart,
Thy life has borne a glorious part.

CAPT. RICHARD C. DERBY.

BY MRS. P. A. HANAFORD.

Fallen to rise !— a hero in the fight ;
  Whose life was given for his country's cause !
Strong in the contest ; battling for the Right ;
  Knowing, in Duty's path, no coward's pause !

Ay! fallen on Antietam's gory field,
  Yet risen to the everlasting heights.
Thy patriotism by thy blood was sealed :
  No weary days for thee, no gloomy nights.

No toilsome marches to the scene of strife ;
  No sore privations in the tented field :
Sweet rest have they who rise to endless life,
  And comforts which no palace home could yield.

Loved friends must mourn him as they watch in vain
   To hear his footsteps sound along the street;
But they shall greet their hero-friend again,
   To part no more, where all God's children meet

Bind, then, around his brow the fadeless bays, —
   " His fame belongeth to his country " now, —
And distant years shall echo back the praise
   Which history shall in truth's clear tones avow.

God help his widowed mother in this hour,
   When heavy seems the stroke his hand hath given !
God bless his lone betrothed one ! — give her power
   To look with faith for union sweet in heaven !

God's smile be on the sister, who no more
   Her childhood's playmate welcomes with delight !
Bid her look upward to that peaceful shore
   Where every heart is glad, and each path bright !

God comfort all the sorrowing ones who sigh
   Because this noble soul hath passed away !
Give them to meet the loved and lost on high,
   Where no dark clouds shall dim the eternal day !

THE END.

www.ingramcontent.com/pod-product-compliance
Lightning Source LLC
Chambersburg PA
CBHW030117030726

47498CB00007B/2435